NOT FOR SALE
261 Brunswick Ave.
Twitter @library 330

PRAISE FOR *DREAMING HOME*

"*Dreaming Home* is nothing short of a conjuring act.
In Kyle, Lucian Childs has created a living, suffering man
out of negative space. Yet we come to know him,
and feel for him, thanks to the cast of funny and flawed
characters whose lives he touches. Through their love,
exasperation, and remorse, the void that is Kyle
miraculously takes on its human shape. Entertaining
and wise, *Dreaming Home* is a wonderful debut."

—CAROLINE ADDERSON, AUTHOR OF
BAD IMAGININGS AND *A HISTORY OF FORGETTING*

"*Dreaming Home* is the propulsive tale of how one act
of cruelty can reverberate through many lives and for
many decades. Childs intricately and carefully brings to
life the constellation of characters who circle around
Kyle and his queer coming of age. *Dreaming Home* poses
brilliant and important questions, forcing the reader to
consider the power we have over one another and
the twisted and painful paths life can take toward joy."

—LYDIA CONKLIN, AUTHOR OF *RAINBOW RAINBOW*

"Both intimate and far-reaching, *Dreaming Home* movingly explores how people change, and how they don't; how they heal, and how they can't ... or maybe still can. There is seemingly no life Childs can't dream his way into, and every character in this beautiful book is drawn with empathy and tenderness."

—CAITLIN HORROCKS,
AUTHOR OF *LIFE AMONG THE TERRANAUTS*

"In *Dreaming Home*, Lucian Childs constructs, from various perspectives, the life of Kyle—a young gay man traumatized early in life, first by his father and then by conversion therapy—who is searching for, as the title suggests, that most elusive of things: home. As he takes us from Texas to San Francisco to Florida, Childs brings it all—compelling prose, first-rate storytelling, and a bittersweet and utterly affecting renegotiation of the meaning of family."

—LORI OSTLUND, AUTHOR OF *AFTER THE PARADE*

"The marvel of Childs' book is its sharp, heartbreaking examination of the true gravity of trauma, extending beyond just the traumatized individual to the friends, family, and lovers beside us. In these six dazzling, entwined stories, he maps their orbits around their damaged polestar. Because of this, it's their collective story—each character's voice amplifying the others—that glows the brightest."

—PATRICK EARL RYAN, AUTHOR OF THE FLANNERY O'CONNOR AWARD-WINNING *IF WE WERE ELECTRIC*

Lucian Childs

Childs

dreaming

home

A JOHN METCALF BOOK

BIBLIOASIS
WINDSOR, ONTARIO

ALWAYS A GIFT

LITTLE FREE LIBRARY

NEVER FOR SALE

Brunswick Ave.
Toronto, ON M5S 2M6
twitter: @library

Copyright © Lucian Childs, 2023

All rights reserved. No part of this publication may be reproduced or
transmitted in any form or by any means, electronic or mechanical,
including photocopying, recording, or any information storage and retrieval
system, without permission in writing from the publisher or a licence from
The Canadian Copyright Licensing Agency (Access Copyright). For an
Access Copyright licence visit www.accesscopyright.ca or call toll free to
1-800-893-5777.

FIRST EDITION
10 9 8 7 6 5 4 3 2 1

Library and Archives Canada Cataloguing in Publication
Title: Dreaming home / Lucian Childs.
Names: Childs, Lucian, author.
Identifiers: Canadiana (print) 20220474451 | Canadiana (ebook) 20220474478
    | ISBN 9781771965491 (softcover) | ISBN 9781771965507 (EPUB)
Subjects: LCGFT: Novels.
Classification: LCC PS8605.H553 D74 2023 | DDC C813/.6—dc23

Edited by John Metcalf
Copyedited by John Sweet
Cover and text designed by Ingrid Paulson

Published with the generous assistance of the Canada Council for the Arts,
which last year invested $153 million to bring the arts to Canadians
throughout the country, and the financial support of the Government of
Canada. Biblioasis also acknowledges the support of the Ontario Arts Council
(OAC), an agency of the Government of Ontario, which last year funded 1,709
individual artists and 1,078 organizations in 204 communities across Ontario,
for a total of $52.1 million, and the contribution of the Government of Ontario
through the Ontario Book Publishing Tax Credit and Ontario Creates.

PRINTED AND BOUND IN CANADA

Affliction is a treasure
and scarce any man hath enough of it.
—John Donne,
Devotions upon Emergent Occasions,
Meditation XVII

For Alex,
always

Rachel

WE WERE HAVING a Natalie Cole spring, that April, my best friend, Tiana, and me. Practically wore the grooves off *Unpredictable*. And we were in junior high. Finally! I was in Math Club, AP Algebra. I turned twelve on the sixteenth and had my first kiss. Everything was totally groovy.

This one day, Ti's dad was driving us home from class after last period. For some reason, they'd stuck us way over at Rancier on the other side of Killeen, so we couldn't walk to school like we'd always done. Her dad's Ram truck was sweet, though. Shiny and red, just off the lot. He'd tricked it out with running lights up front under a shit-eating grille, and chrome ladies lined up on the tailgate with big boobies and high butts.

Ti and me were riding along, singing our heads off with Natalie on the radio. "I've Got Love on My Mind."

We crossed our arms like funky Egyptian goddesses, lifting our hands to the beat, giving our shoulders a little shimmy at the end of each line of the chorus. We *ooooooohed* and *aaaaaahed*, just like her backup singers on the TV.

Ti's dad was the darkest person I ever saw. Not black, the way people say, really, but pretty darn close. The man was built like a brick house. And sweet as all get-out, though sometimes he gave off this hard-core military vibe, like he'd take you out for so much as looking at him.

"Can't go to the Dairy Queen today, girls," he said, turning down the radio. "Got to run errands. I'm buying something nice for Ti's mom. Now keep that on the QT, y'all. It's gonna be crazy special."

Ti and me, we put on our pouty faces, corners of our mouths curved way down and our eyes all boo-hoo and scrunched up.

"Now, don't y'all go making a fuss. I promise, tomorrow we'll do something real nice." He drew that *real* out way long, like train wheels squealing at the bend of a track.

"For instance?" Ti eyeballed her dad all suspicious-like. He wasn't always too good with the follow-through.

I didn't care. He made me laugh. He fought over in Vietnam too, but didn't get captured, like my father did. The army gave Dad some medal, jumped his rank so people started calling him Sergeant Mullen instead of plain old PFC—which was super cool. They'd sent him back from there, though, with a bunch of screws loose. With him, I always had to watch the heck out, 'specially when he was drinking, which, if he wasn't on duty, was tons.

"Y'all tell me what you'd like to do tomorrow," Ti's dad said.

"Double shakes and Big Macs at Mickey D's!" Ti and I screamed at the same time, per usual having a mind meld.

We were barreling toward the army base where both our dads were stationed. Fort Hood. Biggest base in all the US of A. From behind the live oak and the roofs of people's houses came a roar, then a helicopter like the ones Dad piloted cleared the treetops. When my family first moved here, I thought this was groovy. Until he told me they only flew around in circles then came right back and I was like, wah?

Ti, she gave her pops the hairy eyeball when he started going on about that shiftless white boy he'd seen skulking around.

"Sweetheart," he said, amping back up the charm, "you're too young to be dating." Like me, Ti was only twelve.

When he asked me for backup, I was, hey, it's freaking 1977: *I am woman, hear me roar*. But I twiddled a strand of my hair and said in my good-girl voice that a woman ought to always be sensible. Something, of course, I hardly ever was.

When Ti's dad got to the high school, he popped a left. "Let's go check out practice, y'all." He meant varsity football. The man was all in—*Fight Mighty Kangaroos, Fight!* Every at-home game night, for sure you knew where he was. No team on the playing field that day, but the cheerleaders were out practicing their three-tier pyramids. Girls flung themselves off the top, flipped in midair to land on their backs in the arms of waiting boys. Man, I so wanted to be one of those girls, but no way could I muster up that level of trust.

We busted through town—quickie marts, auto parts stores, body shops—and out the other side, where there were open fields again. Top of this rise we could see, way off to the west, the tabletop hills. My dad told me they were over on the San Saba, where the water was cool and clear and real nice. He promised to take me camping there one day. My brother Kyle too, though I don't know why he'd even bother.

"Hey there, house!" Ti and I said as we passed our duplexes, our square, perfectly trimmed yards snug behind their chain-link fences. Saying hey to the house was another thing we'd always done, but now it felt a little dorky.

The truck squealed to a stop in front of the gatehouse. We grabbed our packs from behind the seat back and got out. Ti's dad peeled off.

"Think he's got something going on the side. *Run errands,*" Ti said, making air quotes around the words. "He'll be gone a couple of hours and alls he'll come back with is a stupid bag of chips or something."

I drew *wash me* with my fingertip on the dusty window of the guardhouse. Nobody in it, like always, on account of budget cuts and because there was nothing in our subdivision worth ripping off. *Venable Village,* the sign over the open gate read.

We skipped down the blacktop, holding hands, then broke away. Slowing to a walk, we did a quick look around, hoping nobody saw. We weren't little kids anymore. On either side of the road, under cottonwoods fixing to bust open and make a mess, pickups were parked under carports or run up onto the new lime-green grass.

Me and Ti's duplexes were just like all the rest—white one-story boxes, stretched out like Play-Doh, they were so narrow and long. Our house was teeny—nothing like my grandparents' big, swanky place in Dallas—but I liked it anyway. Had my own room, my treehouse. A screened porch on one side where the nights were cool and nice.

With her key, Tiana let herself into the house next to us. Over at ours, the carport was empty, 'cept for my brother's Schwinn, slumped all sad-looking against one of the supports. The front door was half-open and nobody home—a Mason jar bursting with calla lilies on the dining table the only sign of life. My big brother Kyle would be around someplace, drawing probably. He was three years older than us, but such a spaz. Don't think he had a single friend.

I shut the door to my room, ditched my pack and fell backward onto my bed. That day had been a nightmare. I got detention sixth period for shooting spit wads. Plus, this crazy girl nearly pulled out a bunch of my hair, fighting on the playground. I did call her boyfriend a freaking dork, but still...

Flopped there on my bed, I scanned the trig tables I'd written out in marker on heavy board and tacked to the ceiling. They were the first thing I saw in the morning and the last at night. I thought maybe, if I wasn't so up-in-your-face all the time, Dad would love me, and anything to do with numbers cooled me right down. Turned out I was a big success in math class, which shocked the heck out of everybody, since my grades were mostly the pits.

The low afternoon sun lit up the inside of my little matchbox, making me warm and drowsy. I woke up when Ti squiggled in through my window like she always did, though now she was getting a little too big in the butt. She wore blue jean short-shorts, frayed at the edge, and a tight tank top that showed off her new breasts. The top was a brag meant as a put-down, me having only nubs yet. But I'd started my period already, so, really, she wasn't all that.

She moved her shoulders quick, swinging her teeny purse around and smacking me in the face with it. Plopping down on my bed, she grabbed the copy of *Teen* from my nightstand and leafed through the pages of models in cute skirts and flounced tops. After a bit, she tossed the magazine aside and said, "What do those stuck-up white girls have to do with me? Squat. Rae Rae, let's go get ourselves into some trouble."

Since we were all the way out in Venable Village, our options in the trouble department were pretty much zilch. After a minute, though, I said, "I got it. How about we go find my brother?"

We barged into his room, guns blazing, a couple of lean, mean commandos. He wasn't there, but, taped to the wall above his bed, the portraits he'd sketched glared back at us. My parents, darkly shaded, fingerprint smudges at the edge of the paper. Ti and me popping bubblegum. Our grandparents, penciled in thin, shaky lines. People he'd drawn out of magazines.

Since that was a dud, we ran out behind the house to the patio table. He drew out there sometimes, if it wasn't too hot and the bugs not too bad. But we got diddly.

Ti pointed up with her pinkie finger, mouthing the word *treehouse*. Sure enough, in an opening in the wooden box Dad built in the fork of a bodark, the top of Kyle's head was swiveling back and forth.

Ti and me kicked off our shoes and snuck up the ladder, this time a couple of Special Ops ninjas, climbing real slow and quiet. Ti pulled up the rear, head-butting me in the behind at the top, making me jack-in-the-box partway through the hole in the floor.

Kyle was cross-legged, drawing, hunched over, flopping across his brow that long light-blond hair—strawberry, Mom called it, though I don't know why. His nose was super straight and he had a jaw like the blade of a plow. He was prettier than me by a mile. "Hey, brother," I said, scrambling through the opening. "What's shaking?"

He covered the drawing super quick with his hand and jerked up straight. He was mega tall and nearly bumped his head on the ceiling. His sketchbook was balanced on one knee; on the other was the magazine he was copying. He slapped the magazine closed and crammed it under the sketchbook. Flipped to a fresh page and started penciling the outline of his hand.

"What's it look like I'm doing?"

"Look to me," Ti said, barreling up the ladder, "like you hiding something. What you hiding, Kylie Ky?"

"Nothing." He poked the corner of the mag further under the sketchbook.

"I've got lots of boy cousins," Ti said, crawling inside, "and I can always tell when they lie. They make this funny face. What you think, Rae Rae? Ain't your brother making that face right now?"

"Pretty much."

"And ain't lying a sin, Rae Rae? I know you go to church with your dad."

Kyle's face got all red, a little twitch going on under his right eye. He was sneaking the book and the magazine off his lap and trying to wedge them under his butt.

Ti duckwalked over and snatched the sketchbook from his hand. When Kyle tried to grab it back, it skittered across the floor. The magazine plopped at his feet, on its cover this guy with no shirt on, with a thick mustache and washboard abs. He was buried in sand to just above his crotch.

"Right on," Ti said. "Jackpot!"

She went for the sketchbook. I made a pass at that magazine, but Kyle jerked it out of my fingers and the cover man got torn in two. Half his face leered up from the floorboards. Ti opened the sketchbook and her jaw dropped. She held it up so I could see, started flipping through pages and pages of drawings of naked men, some with big ole hard-ons. I knew what that was, since a neighbor boy showed me his once.

"Gimme that," Kyle said to Ti.

She glowered at him, eyes way squinty, and dropped that book out the window.

"Shit," Kyle said.

"You're so nailed," I said.

Kyle rolled up that mag and snapped it under his armpit. Then he shoved me away and jumped through the opening in the floor. For a big girl, Ti moved super quick, scampering down the ladder like a cat. When I got down, the two of them were having a tug-of-war over the magazine that was getting all crinkly and tore up in their hands.

Ti was super strong too, from pumping iron with her dad, and she pushed Kyle on his ass and the magazine went flying. She caught it by one edge and the centerfold draped down like a curtain. "Holy shit!" Turning the mag around, she showed me this hairy guy in all his glory. "You gonna burn in Hell for this, brother. Isn't that what your good book say, Rae Rae?"

"Oh yeah, big-time. Crispy critters."

My brother scrambled up, cut grass sticking to his T. He tried to snatch the mag from Ti, but she danced away a couple of steps. Rolling it back up and playing like it was a microphone, she sang into it, suddenly getting all Natalie. "Oooh, I've got looooove on my mind. Ain't that right, Kyle? You want these big ole white boys to love you up, don't you?"

"I found it in somebody's trash." Kyle's voice got all serious and deep. He made a run for the sketchbook that was splayed out on the lawn a ways off, and snatched it up. "I just use it for the models, is all. It's called life drawing."

"Life drawing, my ass," Ti said. "You think we're stupid, Kyle? Just 'cause we're little, we don't know what's going on up there?" She held the rolled-up mag at her waist and did the nasty—cupping her hand around the thing and working it up and down real fast, making a face like in a funhouse mirror.

Kyle ran at her like some kind of nut, waving his hands around and opening his eyes mega wide. I stuck out my foot and he tripped, did this little chicken dance before he got right.

"Give it back," he said, his voice suddenly all high. "And don't tell him. Please."

Kyle lunged at Ti again and she tossed me the magazine.

"Rachel, please," he said, and I saw he was crying. For a minute, I almost gave it back. But Ti nabbed the magazine and booked it. In a flash, she was halfway down the block, me tailing behind.

I caught up with her, back of her cousin's place. She was laughing her ass off. "Oooh, snap. That was bad, right?"

"I guess," I said.

Ti's cousin was parked at the picnic table on a little concrete pad, guzzling from a forty of Colt 45. He was so cool, varsity football over at Ellison. Way older than us, but still not legal. Ti dangled the magazine in front of his eyeballs and he reared back, looking as if someone was about to give him a smack.

"Get that shit out of my face. Where you find that nasty-ass thing?"

"Stole it from Kyle."

"For real?"

"For real."

"Man, I always knew the brother was strange."

Ti caught sight of the brown bottleneck poking out of the crumpled paper sack. "Hey, don't bogart the brew, cuz. Gimme some."

"Don't think so. Your dad would fucking flip."

"Well, flip this, mother." Ti held up the mag by one edge and the centerfold flopped out. She mushed it in her cousin's face.

He grabbed Ti by the wrist, wrenched her arm behind her, then pushed her back on the grass. She was laughing. Prancing around, trying to get close enough to smash the glossy pages back in his face.

"Give me a fucking break." He shoved the bottle toward her across the table. "Crazy little bitch."

Ti snatched the bottle and knocked back a swig, then passed it to me.

At Sunday school that week, I got a gold star by my name—Star Rachel Mullen! Recited by heart the whole Lord's Prayer and also 1 Corinthians 13:11–12. I grabbed that forty out of her hand anyway. Didn't want them thinking I was some dweeb. To please Dad, I took little sips when he slipped me his suds, though I hated how bitter it was. This malt liquor actually tasted sweet, so I chugged a bunch. Made me feel like I might barf.

But Ti, she totally got off on it. She was pounding it down, shuffling through the magazine going, "Ooooh, look at that one, Rae Rae." And "Oh my god, this one...What the hell you supposed to do with that?" She slapped the mag shut and flicked it aside. "That's sick, y'all."

Ti's cousin threw his shoulders back, military-like, acting all strict. "Rachel, your brother's a fucking fag."

"Goddam queer," Ti said.

"Yeah," I said. "Stupid pansy."

"Rachel," Ti said, "you're not crying, are you?"

"No, no," I said, grinding my knuckles into my eyeballs. "Got the ragweed, is all."

But I was crying. For my brother, 'cause I knew how it had to go. For whosoever sins does not prosper—one of Dad's favorite verses—but one who confesses and renounces them finds mercy.

How could I go against that? Against God? And my father's wish to have a normal son? Not that it would be a news flash, or anything. It was pathetic to see those two playing catch, Dad going nuts when Kyle practically every time missed the ball. Or to see Kyle sulking, bored out of his gourd, when we went camping.

But doesn't the Bible also say, I am my brother's keeper?

Through the slot between Ti's cousin's and the house next door, I noticed Dad's truck inch into our carport. He and Mom got out, him in his dress blues, his thick mustache neatly trimmed, his flattop freshly cropped. Mom had on her best outfit, her bright-red hair, her strand of pearls popping out against her dark blouse. They were probably back from one of those rah-rah deals on base they always had to go to.

I trudged up the block, psyching myself up and getting all holier-than-thou. I pinched that magazine by a corner, afraid to get contaminated by whatever my brother got on it. The sun had dipped behind the cottonwoods, casting long shadows across the street. In the trees the cicadas were sawing away and a mockingbird mimicked a hawk's call, like it was shrieking a warning.

Dad was waiting at the front door. I lifted up the magazine, the centerfold tumbling back out, and told him. On Dad's face, a pained look broke out into a sneer, then into a full-blown Halloween monster mask. He stormed through the house, but my brother wasn't there. Not in the backyard either. Or the treehouse. His bike had disappeared.

My father scrambled back into his truck and squealed off. As Mom and I were finishing supper, he came back empty-handed and told her she better call the cops. Within minutes, red-and-blue lights were spinning out front and a good ole boy, whose belly hung over his belt, was at the door taking a description.

Around midnight, the policeman was back with Kyle in handcuffs, just to scare some sense into him, Dad told me later. The cop picked up my brother at a rest stop on I-35 trying to hitch a ride south. When the officer asked Kyle where in the heck was he running to, all Kyle said was, away.

After the cop sped off, Dad yanked Kyle by his long hair into the living room and started whaling on him. Not with the belt, like usual, but his fists. I couldn't stand it and ran out. Ever since I was seven, I practically lived at Ti's place, so my feet found their way over there.

Ti was at her bedroom window looking over at our house. She had her arms wrapped tight around her and it seemed like maybe she was shaking. We stood side by side, not close enough to touch but connected by what we'd done, by each cry coming through the opening, by the sound of each whack of the fist. And it was as if the ground under our feet opened up, the distance between us suddenly big as the ocean I saw once with Mom on the Gulf. And though I pushed them out of my head, the images kept coming back—what our fathers must have done to people during the war.

It was real quiet in our house by the time I dared go over there. In the back, my parents huddled in the dark around the patio table, Mom crying in her hands, Dad staring off, looking even more spaced-out than usual. On the table between them, a stack of black books. Kyle's sketchpads, probably full of drawings of naked guys.

When I slunk back to my room, Kyle's door was cracked open. I could just make him out in the night-light, on his back in bed, that light-blond hair making him seem like an old man. A bruise smudged his cheek and there was the start, too, of a real bad black eye. Blood ran from his nose and pooled on his upper lip. It was so weird, him lying there still as stone, staring at the ceiling without even blinking, all the drawings on the wall gawking down at him like people looking in an open casket at a funeral.

I should have said something, but everything I came up with sounded like a lie. So I slouched back to my room, threw myself in bed and buried my head in my pillow like those big, stupid birds do in the cartoons, trying to make everything go away.

But my mind kept seeing stuff. What was left of us, wearing black, riding in the back of a limo and single-filing it to the cemetery with a bunch of other cars behind. Mom was sniffling into her handkerchief. Beside her, me and Dad transformed. Me, snugged in his arms, now his prim darling and only child. Him, the fun dad again, the one Mom talked about, the one I saw laughing in pictures taken in Korea, before I got born and he was sent off to fight in Vietnam.

My brother's bloody face floated up too, and the words printed in my Bible under a picture of a weeping man: *Listen! Your brother's blood cries out to me. And so, cursed shall you be.*

AND JUST AS GOD SAID, after that everything fell apart.

Kyle got grounded, confined to quarters. They didn't even let him go to school, much less leave the house, afraid people would get a look at his swollen face, all spotted with purplish blue. At night, when no one would notice, Mom let Kyle walk around in the backyard. I'd be at the dining table with my homework and would see him out there near the chain-link fence by the highway. He'd be hoofing it side to side across the yard or else just standing there, a shadow lit up by the headlights of passing cars. After a while, Mom would call him and he'd slink back to his room.

They wouldn't allow me in there, which was a relief, really. I mean, what would I say to him? Mom served him his food on a TV tray at the foot of his bed and sometimes she would eat her meal with him or just nibble on the Mission figs she loved. I'd listened to them in there from my room. Sometimes he'd be crying. Sometimes the two of them shared secrets late into the night. I couldn't get what they said, but it made me real mad. She never talked with me like that.

Once, Dad stormed into Kyle's room, all hopped-up on beer. Mom ran out and stood by me in the hall. And Dad, he got down on his knees and prayed over Kyle, 'cause in my opinion he truly feared for his son, his only begotten. Then Dad paced beside the bed, reciting verses from the Bible that was flopped open in his hand.

"Whoever conceals their sin, does not prosper."

Dad shuffled through the tabs he'd stuck on the thin pages and found another good one. "Put to death whatever belongs to your earthly nature. Because the wrath of God is coming."

And saving the best for last, he spouted First Corinthians, the one everybody knows. "You are not your own; you were bought at a price. Therefore honor God with your body."

Kyle, he just lay there through all that, staring up at the ceiling like maybe he'd tacked trig tables up there too.

Weeks passed and sometimes it seemed as if Dad wanted to beg Kyle's forgiveness for beating him so bad. Minutes later, Dad acted like he was fixing to rough Kyle up all over again. The pastor from our church came to the house after dinner a couple of times and talked to Dad, while Mom sat in the corner wringing her hands. Some bigwig from a program near Waco even visited. Late one night, I shuffled into the kitchen for a glass of milk or something and found Dad at the table, head down, bottle of beer in one hand, his open Bible in the other. Those color tabs sticking out everywhere marked his favorite passages on sin, retribution, repentance, death.

Beginning of May, my brother was gone. At first my parents told me he was off at camp, but I was like, no, school's still going on. Then it was a special academy where he was at. And I said, special how? And why didn't I get to go? Finally, they said I should just shut up about it.

That summer, Dad and I went camping a bunch, not over on the San Saba, but taking his ATV and pitching a tent in the cedars at the lake just outside town. Also, we took up bowling. Also golf. Anything to stay away from that duplex and Mom.

She started really putting on the pounds. Drinking too, something I'd never seen her do much. Dad, he went cold turkey right after Kyle left. Guess he and Pastor had been praying on it for some time. It was crazy, 'cause Dad kind of mellowed after he quit, whereas when Mom started boozing, you never knew what the heck would set her off.

Like this one time after dinner, we were having dessert and watching TV on the screened porch. Except for Sundays, we had the evening meal out there, the ceiling fan doing double time and getting all wobbly. The dinner table sure looked lonesome, no calla lilies, no us.

That evening, Dad was still in his fatigues, T. MULLEN stitched in a white band on the green cloth. He positioned himself on our big L-shaped couch at the end of the y-axis. Mom was getting hammered on red wine all the way down at the end of the x-axis, sitting as far away from Dad as she could. She'd just dyed her red hair a pitch-black, out of protest, she said. Whatever that meant.

At the top of the hour, after the deodorant commercial came on, she made a show of eating one of her Mission figs, biting into the jelly bag, slowly nipping off the stem. "How about watching *Masterpiece Theatre?*" she said. Like she really cared what we thought.

Me, I was perched behind my TV tray in the quilted right angle of the L, at (0,0) as if I couldn't plot where I was on the curve between them. Before it had time to melt, I shoveled my Neapolitan ice cream down so fast it made my teeth hurt. I only ate the chocolate part, the vanilla and strawberry in my bowl just a pink mess.

Through the window, Dad looked out at our backyard that he kept square and crisp as Astroturf with the lawn mower he liked to ride around on. "Isn't it time for *The Rockford Files?*"

Her pinkie finger extended, Mom popped another fig into her mouth. She narrowed her eyes and said how she should have stayed in Dallas after high school and gone for that banker, like her father wanted. Bankers had taste. Surely the one in Dallas preferred British theater over a silly detective show with that idiot person, James Garner.

Dad said, well okay then. His voice getting all gushy, he complimented her on her new dye job, on her dress that was actually more like a tent than a piece of clothing. I felt so sorry for him. I could see what it cost, as if he had to rouse himself to crawl out of a very deep hole.

As if things couldn't get any worse, sometime around then Ti started hanging out tons with her cousin, always forgetting to ask me to come with. I heard them down there behind his house yukking it up all the time. Beginning of August, her dad got orders to ship out to Fort Benning. Georgia, she told me. We promised to call or write, but I knew we probably never would.

NOW GOD, HE PUT the final nail in the coffin Labor Day weekend. We were supposed to drive up to my grandparents' in Dallas for the big Turner family party. Grandmother Elaine's shindigs were famous. I remember them from when I was little, the time we lived up there with them when Dad was at the war. I followed Grandmother around then like a baby chick. She was such a hoot, always cracking wise in her singsongy East Texas accent. Granddad C.K. called her a firecracker, I guess 'cause she had bright-red hair like my mom.

But as I said, God had other plans.

A couple days before we were going to drive to Dallas, Mom said, because Kyle was still at the religious academy or whatever, she and Dad were nixing the whole trip. My guess: Dad had nothing to do with it. I didn't get why Kyle not being there meant we all had to bail on the deal. Guess it was what the Sunday school teacher called penance, which was stupider than crap.

Labor Day morning, I was spread-eagled on my bed, about to boil over. To tamp things down, I stared up at the constellation of trig tables and memorized cosines, increasing their angles by increments of one. Cos 0° = 1.00. Cos 1° = 0.9998. Cos 2° = 0.9994. Then 0.9986, 0.9976, 0.9962, 0.9945. I drilled up to Cos 12°, then Mom came in, taking a breather from ruining the dinner she'd planned.

She had a paperback book snuggled under one arm, in one hand a coffee cup of red wine, in the other a bowl of Mission figs. She forgot again to put on her makeup, so you could see the freckles polka-dotting her pale face. Those spots were top secret usually, she wore so much pancake. She was dressed in that flowing muumuu thing—a purple sack of cotton cloth—to hide all the weight she'd put on. Now my brother and I could take care of ourselves, she didn't do much but nibble all day. Her figs, but mostly just chips and stuff. Since Kyle shipped off, it got way worse. It was like, if she ate all the time, she wouldn't have to think about what they were doing to him up there.

She placed the bowl on my nightstand, took a fig by its little brown stem and bit into the flesh. For her, I tried to like them. The sweetness was nice, the hint of cinnamon and vanilla, but they were rubbery and gritty in a way I couldn't stand.

Lowering herself onto the bed beside me, she cleared her throat, so I knew I was about to get a talking-to. She eyed the posters on my wall that I'd gotten the year before.

One from *Rocky* that I'd snagged at the premiere up in Dallas. And a "Jimmy Carter for President" poster with a black-and-white photo of his squinty-eyed self.

Mom pointed at Jimmy. "You understand I come from a long line of Republicans, don't you? Your grandfather was state chairman. Twice, I believe."

I shrugged my shoulders, but I knew. Why I put the poster up in the first place.

"Do you even know who the man is?"

"He's president. Duh!" I rolled my eyes.

"I mean what he stands for." She sipped from the mug; already her teeth were stained a reddish gray.

On TV the year before, Jimmy had talked a lot about fighting corruption, so I said that.

Her paperback was splayed on one knee. On the cover was this shirtless man with a huge pillowy chest and long silver hair. He'd fit right in, if he was naked, in Kyle's magazine.

"I suppose the president is trying to do the right thing. That Watergate stuff was a mess. I bet you figured you were doing the right thing too. Didn't you, Rachel?" My mother sucked another fig into her mouth, sliced into the pulp and twisted off the stem. "But what do you know? You're just a child."

To keep from messing up her words, when she got tipsy like this, she slowed way down her usual Texan—that quick, closed-mouth way of speaking—and started sound-

34

ing all Southern Belle, sort of like Grandmother Elaine. "An shouldna chile be forgivun?"

I wasn't sure who she was asking. Not me. Jimmy maybe, who I knew also was born again.

I said the only thing I could think of. "Suffer the little children, for they…"

She waved the mug in my face, wine splashing over the lip, making a red splotch on my carpet. "I've had it with you two preaching at me from the Bible. That book is filled with nothing but hate."

"Mom! People go to Hell for saying stuff like that."

"And you think I'm not there already?"

She got over-the-top like that when she was drunk, but I knew what she meant. Living in our tiny house, marrying a man who turned into someone else. A son lost and she didn't raise a finger to stop it.

"I wish I could take it back," I said.

Mother drew me close. Under the tang of red wine was the smell of figs, all cinnamony and vanilla. She pulled my head onto her bosom's rise and fall. I heard the rumble of her breath, the thumping of her beating heart.

"Do you, really? Treacherous child."

The Boys
at the Ministry

Let the redeemed of the Lord tell their story.

When we're told to get Pastor Williams, we so know where to find him: on the loading dock behind the Ministry. With broken pallets and grody fifty-five-gallon barrels, there he is—hanging out on a white plastic food service bucket, staring off at our industrial park. Since our old Faith Leader, Brother Price, got canned, Pastor's out here lots. His eyes all puffy and red. He tells us it's allergies, but we know it's not.

'Cause we miss Brother Price too. Our old Faith Leader was a real string bean, but with a little paunch he would rub whenever he laughed. A super straight-shooter—never wrote us up just 'cause he had his shorts twisted in a knot over something. Snuck us chocolates after lights out.

Called us Sunshine and, when he led morning sing, always picked out happy songs.

Lot of us have been with men like that. They buy us games for our Ataris. Their kisses taste like mouthwash and booze. They blow us in the backseats of their cars and never ever give up their phone numbers. Afraid we'll rat them out to the cops, when all we want is to take their broken hearts in our hands.

Sitting on his little plastic throne, Pastor Williams catches sight of us and turns to the side to wipe his eyes. He's a porker—like the Skipper on *Gilligan's Island*—plump cheeks, a couple of chins. His shirt can't hardly hold him. He beams at us boys all lined up perfect on the concrete slab, just like those bay doors on the opposite loading dock.

"Ah," he says, "the Blessed Ones."

We boys from godly families. Section heads in our church choirs, Bible Study leaders, next-gen pastors. We were that. The Lord taketh away. Blessed be the Lord.

"Sir, yes, sir." Brother Stalwart snaps his right hand under the brown mop that springs from the middle of his head, like the parting of the Red Sea in Exodus. He clutches a Bible with tons of colored tabs sticking out. Go toe-to-toe with him on chapter and verse and you're dead.

"You've got the fire, son," Pastor says. "Jesus knows you are his foot soldier."

A wind, weirdly cold for the beginning of October, smashes into us. We shiver in our thin white dress shirts and khaki pants. The metal door behind us clicks, whistles for a sec then whooshes open. Brother Mullen walks onto the narrow landing.

He's a tall, broad-shouldered boy. Good-looking, too, though we try not to stare for fear we'll get all warm and mushy inside. But he's super scrawny, bug-eyed—maybe fasting way more than us, so great are his sins. His rusty-blond hair curls down past his earlobes. The length is really pushing it, but Pastor says it's okay. Probably feels sorry for the kid, who's been at the Ministry longer than anyone.

The story how he got here has been passed from boy to boy. Mullen's dad—a ten-foot-tall ogre in combat fatigues, blood dripping from pointy teeth, US ARMY tattooed on his forehead—dragged his son across the asphalt and dumped him at the Ministry's front door like a sack of trash.

Never hear Mullen grousing, though. He's thankful to be here, just like we are. For scripture says boys such as us ought to be stoned to death. That's the Number One Bible verse that calls us to be delivered from the empty way of life. In all, there are five, bull's-eyed at our iniquities.

Brother Mullen scuffles to the front of the loading dock.

"Yes, brother?" Pastor stares over the edge into the pit.

"It's time for the meeting. I was told to remind you by Faith Leader Bennett."

A replacement for Brother Price—as if!—Brother Bennett is our new Faith Leader. His daddy's pastor at the huge church in Waco that runs the Ministry.

"Oh, yes. Now the great endeavor begins," Pastor says, all smiley, puffing out his chest so big we think it's going to bust. "Brothers, you remind me of myself as a boy. Like you, I was just so excited to be chosen for Heartland Christian. Lordy, you're about to attend the finest parochial school in all of Texas. And the best part...they really want you. Some of y'all come from places that don't. I witness how you suffer and are put upon. I suffer too. Y'all know that. But through our trials we are brought closer to Christ and there we see everything anew."

He points to the trash blowing in circles below the dock—paper sacks, plastic tops with their straws sticking out like little sails that lost their boats. "Brother Mullen, you see that now, don't you?"

The scrawny blond boy peers over the edge, lining the toes of his shiny patent leathers on its metal lip. "Yes, Pastor. They are being moved by His unseen hand."

Another whistle and whoosh. Faith Leader Bennett's in the open doorway, his skin pale as the pages of the Bible strapped to his hip. On a chain around his neck is the cross he welded together out of pipe fittings after he was redeemed. "Pastor. Brothers. If you all would honor us with your presence."

He stands aside, motioning down the hallway behind him with one hand, his other throttling his pipe cross, like he's trying to snap its freaking neck.

WE SKITTY ON DOWN to the small meeting room for the confab. Not with those losers ogling us through the window, but just us Heartland boys. We are, like, super psyched!!!!!!! By our own efforts and by the blood of Jesus Christ, WE HAVE BEEN SAVED. Well, not to the max. We still got "proclivities," as Pastor calls them. But it's like we're about to pop the tail of our skateboards. We're ready to jump and catch air, y'all!

We've prayed for this ever since we saw the demon in the mirror, felt him slither down and strike us in the crotch. His poison oozed out a dank heat, made our limbs heavy, made us touch ourselves and think of other boys.

Pastor Williams waddles in, a smile plastering over the sad face he had on before. Faith Leader Bennett skulks behind him into the room and starts patrolling the perimeter, slinking first one way then doubling back quick. He eyes us while we set up our folding chairs in a circle. Some of us sneaked in to see *Star Wars* right before we got sent here. Since Faith Leader Bennett dresses in black and is always barking orders, they call him Darth Vader behind his back.

When everyone gets settled, Pastor Williams takes a chair in front of the blackboard. "Oh, boys. You have come so far. We're expecting breakthroughs of the spirit here and you have not disappointed."

He flashes us a Heartland Christian Academy brochure. On the cover, a lion holding a shield and a sword and a photo of three smiley white boys. "We've promised your parents while you're here at the Ministry that we'll not scrimp on your education. This is a thing, however, Faith Leader Bennett and I aren't prepared to provide. So we've made a special arrangement with the Academy, just for you Blessed Ones." Pastor's eyes glisten and his voice gets all buttery. "Oh, boys. Just pass this one last test and you can return to your families' loving arms. Finish the semester with good grades at Heartland Christian and do *not* get caught doing any nasty stuff."

Faith Leader Bennett steps into the middle of the circle and bows his head. "For whosoever sins sexually, sins against their own body."

That one there is the Number Two Bull's-Eye verse. 1 Corinthians 6:18.

Faith Leader runs a finger along the little caterpillar on his upper lip we call his *stache*. He's twenty-three, maybe twenty-four, with black hair and busy eyebrows. His daddy started the Ministry ten years back when he caught Faith Leader Bennett in the church sacristy sucking face with another boy.

He starts in on how we're going to board all week at Heartland, then get brought back here end of Friday, *blah blah*. Bible Study all weekend, *blah blah*. Trauma Reenactment, *blah*. Foundations of Masculinity class.

We're not listening. He pretty much told us this already. He just likes to hear himself talk, since he's such a freaking Important Person.

"Can I hear an Amen, brothers?"

44

We perk up and shout, so we don't cross him.

"As you know, I was healed of sexual brokenness right here at the Ministry. Went to Heartland too, and passed the test. And praise Jesus, for he has given me natural affection for the woman. Last year, my wife and I became as one flesh."

That's Number Three, so we shout hallelujah. We want that with all our hearts, really, but it kind of grosses us out.

"I'm going to let you boys in on a secret," Faith Leader says. "You know, Pastor believes sometimes change isn't possible, that our faith struggle will get us through the Pearly Gates."

Pastor squirms in his chair like a kid that got sent to the principal.

"Adherence to natural law may be out of reach for some. But not for you, brothers. You *can* change. But you got to heed Jesus when he says: if any man would come after me, let him deny himself and take up the cross. What I'm saying is, there's certain thoughts you got to say no to. They may be your cross, but they are not you. Any questions?"

We just sit there, gawking at our hands folded in our laps. Saying no to our thoughts is pretty much all we ever do.

"Well then, who'd like to share from their Record of Trespasses?"

Oh man, we're so busted. Most of us left our composition books back in our bunks. But Brother Stalwart jumps up, his handsome face lit up like crazy, his muscles bulging under his shirt. He waves his black notebook around, grunting like a pig at a trough.

Brother Taggart—a light-skinned Black boy from somewhere near the Louisiana border—he stands too, holding his book real high. He rolls his eyes way back in his head. It blows us away how much he takes God in.

Faith Leader motions Taggart into the center of the circle, then stalks out between two folding chairs and starts back up his pacing. Stalwart sinks down in his seat all sour-faced, like a star quarterback who's just been benched.

Brother Taggart's only fourteen, but built like a fire plug and mega strong, his shaved head shiny like a spit wad. His folks put him in that place in Mississippi the cops shut on account of the seriously bad stuff that went on there. Electrocuting his dick while they flashed pics of guys getting it on, doping him up, isolation cells, stun guns, whips. But what he shares in these sessions, he lets on later, he's mostly made up.

We do that too. 'Cause unless we confess the many times we were molested, we'll never be free of unwanted same-sex attraction. But pretty much, we got zip. A couple of puny blow jobs. Plus getting fag-bashed some, which doesn't count. It's just the wages of sin, y'all.

But Taggart, that squat Black boy's a friggin' Hemingway. He's scrawled pages and pages in his Record with sins he hasn't even committed. They're super convincing. We didn't know there were so many ways to take a penis inside yourself.

"Brothers, I need a witness." Taggart's voice is getting deep, not like a man's yet, but on the way. He talks slow, like they do in East Texas, dragging out his words and adding extra stuff.

Amen, we say, and lean way in, 'cause we know this is going to be good.

"Harken to me and weep. When I was eight, this man down the way, a special friend of my mom's, if you catch my drift, he says he's going to be my special friend too. He leads me into the woods back of our house. I get real excited 'cause he says he's taking me to this secret spot. But we get there, it's nothing but a clearing with a bunch of stumps. He parks me down on one, strips my pants to my ankles and rapes me to kingdom come.

"Now, this wasn't no ordinary man. Ask me how I know? 'Cause when he was reaming me out, his eyes glowed red and these two little horns popped out his skull. As he came, 'twas the voice of Beelzebub himself, declaring he'd come to claim me."

We are mega tripping now, eyes wide, jaws practically on the floor. For sure, he's gone too far with this one. He's riffing the good stuff, hoping they'll spring him so he can split to San Fran and suck cock, like he brags about. But Pastor's nodding like a bobble-head and Faith Leader's grin is like the Joker's in that old *Batman* TV show.

Snap. Again, Snap. It's bug-eyed Brother Mullen. Faith Leader told the tall blond boy he'd better wear a rubber band around one wrist to pluck whenever he had unclean thoughts. By now, the skin there is all raw and red.

47

THEY'VE PUT ALL US Heartland boys in the same dormitory. Usual deal, though. Windowless room, this one smelling dusty, like the janitor's closet it was only a week ago. Bunks from the concrete floor to the tile ceiling. Fluorescent lights humming overhead like God's telling us something. But it's all *eeeeezzzzzuuuuubbbaaaawaaana*. Even those of us who speak in tongues can't figure out that mess.

We're way off from the other kids. Close as us Heartland boys are to perfect sexual health, Pastor doesn't want those dickwads contaminating us. They act like the sinners they are in their one-on-ones with Pastor. They clam up and don't repent for all their diddling. They flunk their test for spiritual intelligence and moral insight.

Brother Mullen takes a seat on a lower bunk. He opens his composition book and starts drawing Brother Taggart, who's eyeballing the open door like he's about to make a run for it. Faith Leader steps out into the hall, shuts the door behind him. We need to go to the john, we ring the bell, he says through the narrow vertical slot. Case anyone's tempted to mess around, there are cameras at two corners.

When Taggart hears Faith Leader's keys jiggling in the lock, the bald boy rushes over, grabs the handle and tries to yank the door off.

"Hey," Faith Leader says, "you need to piss?"

Taggart shakes his head.

"Well then, get in your bunk," Faith Leader says, then disappears down the hall.

Squat Brother Taggart shuffles backward over to the rear wall, the whole time keeping a bead on that door. Then BAM!—he's whaling on the wall with his fists.

We gawp at those cameras. Their little red eyes never blink once.

BAM! Taggart hammers the nubby concrete block again. If he doesn't take a chill pill, he's going to blow it for everybody. They'll call off the whole Heartland deal and we'll never get out of this dump.

Brother Mullen, mouth open, bug-eyes extra wide, he's shaking his leg so bad, the whole bunk is quaking. He drops his pencil into the slot at the center of his book, reaches out and tugs the hem of the Black boy's shirt. But Taggart doesn't notice and is rearing back, about to head-butt the wall.

"Brother Taggart. Friend. Will you lead us in the evening prayer?"

Swooping in to save the day, it's muscly Brother Stalwart. Seriously, that's his actual last name. His parents took it when the family got born again. It's mop-topped Stalwart who usually leads our prayers. He's probably as tripped out as us, though, by the little red eyes in the corners and by the blood Taggart's stamping onto the wall.

"Right on, brother," Taggart says. "Mix it up, right?"

The whole room sighs, 'cause we've been practically holding our breaths the whole time.

Taggart slides a bloody hand across his chrome dome. "Let us bow our noggins. Lord, my soul is, like, super bummed. Pump me up with your Word, Bro. Keep me from my piss-poor ways and teach me how to get down with you."

Holier-than-thou Stalwart squashes up his handsome face, like maybe he just swallowed battery acid. He flicks the tabs on his Bible with his thumb and they make a fluttery bird's wing sound. "You mocking his Word, Taggart?"

"Just bringing it to the masses. Jesus has armed me with the facts. I got some big-time loaves and fishes shit, y'all."

Snap. Snap. It's Brother Mullen with the rubber band taking a little torture break from his sketching. Shaded in the journal on his lap, Brother Taggart's face is staring back—the big lips and broad nose, the baby fat that still clings to his cheeks.

Static on the intercom, then Faith Leader's voice is electron-beamed into our skulls. "You all supposed to be using this time for contemplation. In your bunks with your flash cards, now!"

We dive into our cribs, lean our heads against the cold block wall and thumb through our three-by-fives where we've scratched down the Bull's-Eyes.

Snap, again. From the back of the room. Snap. Then quiet. And, whispered real soft, Brother Taggart says, "I'm okay now. Please stop."

+ + +

AFTER BREAKFAST the next morning, we grab our duffels and line up outside in the well of the loading dock next to the Ministry's old minibus. We're shivering bad. Our arms wrapped tight around us, we stomp the cold from our patent leathers onto the dusty pavement. There's the sound of geese honking their way to the Gulf, their lazy Vs dotting the sky lightening toward the horizon. Right above us, though, it's as dark as a new pair of jeans.

Brother Stalwart is at the front, lording it over us with his perfect hair, his muscles, his good looks. Taggart and Mullen slouch at the back. The Black boy, who is way shorter, gets up on his toes and whispers something in Mullen's ear. Mullen starts a smile but shoves it back down and plucks the rubber band at his wrist.

The bus doors swivel open and we file in and stow our duffels in the overhead racks.

"Let us pray," Pastor says at the front of the bus.

We kneel in the aisle, one hand on our knee, the other frozen to a seat's shiny top rail. We recite the verse along with Pastor. "Oh Lord, you know my follies; the wrongs I have done are not hidden from you."

It's the first time we've spoken all morning and the words are gravelly in our mouths. In case we forget them, they're painted in gold, old-timey letters on the panel above the windshield.

We plop down on our seats, mindful not to sit next to anyone lest it lubricate the proclivities. The brownnoser Stalwart situates himself in the front row so Pastor can get a good look at his total hotness. He opens his Bible at a blue tab, draws his finger down the tight columns of text while he reads.

Taggart sprawls out in the back bench, his eight ball glistening in the overheads. He rubs a frowny face into the frost etched on the inside of the glass. Mullen perches in the row directly in front of him and twirls a strand of blond hair around one finger.

The rest of us boys press our palms into the seats' thin foam and, like reading Braille in the beads of hardened gum underneath, try to make out messages from those who came before us.

Pastor Williams gets comfy in the driver's seat. He's wearing his old Heartland Christian school tie so tight, his fat face is lobster red. Faith Leader pounces onto the bus last, the creases of his black clothes sharp as knives. He points at each of us one by one, doing his count. When he gets to the back, he orders Mullen to move up. "I'm seeing you and Taggart together a little too much."

On Pastor's fourth try, the engine cranks. He wrangles the stick into first and heads out. Through the jittery back window, in the dim light, we glimpse our industrial park. It's way outside town, far from the prying eyes, Pastor says, of the secular humanists who've royally screwed everything up. There's a row of five semis. Porta-potties lined up like dominoes ready to get flicked over. Dead weeds busting out of the asphalt.

Humble as our home may be, Pastor reminds us, everything leads us to worship and joy in the Creator. Watching it grow smaller behind us is like seeing ourselves from outside our bodies. Pretty soon we won't even be able to tell it's there.

Pastor glances up at us in the rearview. "Y'all understand how we have labored to set this up at Heartland Christian? You can't be like those three we sent over there last semester. Not even a month and they get caught with their pants down. And I do not mean that metaphorically." He shakes his head so hard, we think maybe it'll turn all the way round like that girl in *The Exorcist*.

Brother Stalwart shoots up at his seat in front. He places his hand on his muscly chest as if he's about to say the Pledge of Allegiance. "You shall not lie with a man as a woman. It is an abomination."

That's Number Four. This Bull's-Eye will for sure get a person deep-fried in Hell.

We slump in our seats, but not so much that Faith Leader will notice and write us up. We're just super tired, is all, what with being waked up all through the night for prayers. Pastor catches us wilting in the rearview, but like our old Faith Leader, Brother Price, he doesn't make a big deal about it. Just rolls over the rumble strip to rattle us back to attention.

Vibrations spark up our spines. All of a sudden, we're freaking super bad, scared we'll turn out like those three backsliders, swamped by our proclivities. Afraid Faith Leader will bounce us back with the losers and yank our commissary privileges—no candy bars or Cokes. No five-year-old copies of *Teen World* magazine. We don't give a hoot what happened back in 1972, but at least it's something to read other than the Bible.

And, for sure, we don't want to lose our parents' mail, though a bunch gets blacked out. Faith Leader's super careful not to let our folks pass on any negative influences. We get that they're a big reason for our problem, but we miss them anyway. We're starting to forget what they look like. Are our mothers' eyes blue or brown? Did they take that class they were talking about? Are our fathers making our sisters play catch because we're not around and we never liked it anyway?

Pastor loosens his tie and the color in his face begins to fade. He starts up the heater. Like, finally! We're turning into Popsicles back here. The windows fog over. The bus smells of rusty nails and old socks.

"Remember to smile a lot when you get to the Academy," Pastor's reflection tells us in the mirror. "You got a joy inside now that can't be taken away by circumstance. For whosoever believes, rivers of living water flow within them. Who can tell me what that passage means?"

"Ooh, ooh." Brother Stalwart is about to bust a gut, his smug face getting all red.

"Anybody else?" Pastor says.

Brother Stalwart grunts. This All-American Boy's got the living waters thing nailed. As proof, the Lord smears a toothy grin ear to ear, that's way creepy.

"Anybody?"

If Stalwart raises his Bible any higher, his arm's going to pop out of its socket. Pastor looks kind of droopy-faced. "Go ahead, then, son."

Brother Stalwart hugs his Bible and gawks at the ceiling as if he's checking his cheat sheet. "It means make a joyful noise unto the Lord."

"Why, that's right. You can't get that from any book. Not even the Bible. You know it in your heart. Go ahead. Try it, boys. Make a joyful noise."

We stare out the windows. A Mickey D's slides by. A Taco Bell. A 7-Eleven. We totally flip—we all want Slurpees so bad!

From his station at the front of the bus, Faith Leader grips his pipe cross like it's a light saber. "You heard Pastor. Make a joyful noise, people."

Hallelujah, we say, but it's as if we're glued to the boob tube watching *The Waltons* and our moms just asked us how our day went.

"A joyful noise right now!" Faith Leader's face gets all twisted. He squeezes his cross like he really is Darth Vader and he's going to rip it off its chain, make it go whoosh and slice us all in half with its ruby-red flame.

We holler something, making like the fans at those football games our fathers drag us to. Only scrawny-assed Brother Mullen doesn't make a peep, just gazes straight ahead, all zombie-like. Snap goes his rubber band. Snap.

Faith Leader's got a hard-on for him, big-time—striding down the aisle, clutching and unclutching his hand. "Brother Mullen," he yells in the tall boy's ear.

Nothing.

He hollers the boy's name again.

The kid looks off, his bug-eyes all Virgin Mary, as if the sadness of the whole freaking planet's rolled up in those two little balls.

"Kyle Mullen, you will answer me."

Mullen swivels around and gazes up at Faith Leader. It almost seems there's tears in the boy's eyes. Nobody probably called him by his first name since forever.

"A joyful noise or give me twenty."

Nothing.

Faith Leader yanks his hand up. Since he got to the Ministry, he's already smacked Mullen once that we know of, though Pastor told him he couldn't.

In the back, squat Brother Taggart slams his fist into his seat, leaving a big old dint in the vinyl.

"It's not too late to mess this up, Taggart," Faith Leader says, "if that's what you're figuring."

Brother Mullen glances back and shines the Mother Mary on Taggart. Then he shoves past Faith Leader into the aisle and crouches on the floor mat. His long blond hair flops across his face. His push-ups are by the book: flat back, his chicken-neck arms tucked at his sides. He doesn't even break a sweat. When he gets up, the mat's dug grooves into the palms of his hands.

Snap. We hear it and icicles slide up our backs. Snap.

"Sit your ass down," Faith Leader says.

"Brother Bennett," Pastor says from behind the steering wheel. "We appreciate your enthusiasm, but why don't we take it down a notch."

"You coddle him, Pastor. Boy's been here too long. The Council needs to see some improvement."

In the rearview, Pastor's eyeballs jerk around in their sockets for a sec, then he shoots us a nervous smile. The Council's up in Waco—Faith Leader's daddy and some other men—who Pastor's in hot water with on account of Brother Price.

We wish more than ever Brother Price was back. Nobody'd be doing push-ups now. We'd be singing "Sipping Cider through a Straw" or something. Brother Price, he'd turn his big eyes on us, as if he was X-raying our noggins. He'd pray for us and lay his hand on our shoulders. We hadn't been touched for so long, we nearly lost it.

Guess he did some laying of hands on Pastor too. We'd hear them behind the closed office door, talking about faith

57

and how with God's love everything is possible. About the latest Rangers game or what place had the best barbecue. Then it'd get super quiet and we'd go back to our bunks and cry and wish we didn't know what they were up to.

One day, somebody from the Council showed up. Skinny guy, looking like Ichabod Crane, spouting Bible passages even Brother Stalwart never heard of. The guy babysat us while Pastor and Brother Price went to some deal up in Waco. When Pastor came back, Brother Price wasn't with him. In a few days, our new Faith Leader showed up with his black clothes and his pipe cross. After that, Brother Price's name was only ever whispered by us.

The sky's washed out to robin's egg toward the horizon. It's scratched up with wispy clouds and long, feathery airplane trails that make us think of powdered sugar and french fries. The bus turns off the Interstate and soon we're grinding down suburban streets—brick houses with peaked roofs and turquoise swimming pools out back.

A gust of wind slaps the side of the minibus. Windows rattle in their frames, letting in cold puffs with a Christmassy smell of woodsmoke. We want so bad to get zapped by the straight gun, to be one of the boys in those houses. They don't worry about seeing demons in their mirrors. They throw make-out parties with girls, weekend nights their folks are out. They know everything there is about cars. They swipe their dad's lesbo porn and watch it on their brand new VHS players. We want to chill on their porches until those dads call us to dinner. Or watch the sisters dance on the lawn to ABBA songs on their portable radios.

Brother Mullen testified once that when he ragged on his sis for narcing him out to their dad about this porn mag, she was like, had to, bro. It's the due penalty of your perversion. Bull's-Eye Number Five! Girl's got her scripture down cold!

THE BUS BUSTS out onto a wide road—three lanes on either side of a meridian lined with bare-branched, broken trees. About a half mile away, there's the dark shape of this huge church. The cross on top of the steeple lights up gold in the rays of the rising sun.

In the rearview, Pastor's eyes twinkle like his mom just handed him a treat. "Behold, this is the land I promised."

He slips the minibus behind the line of cars that's crawling in stops and starts toward the school drop-off zone a block off. We stand up and begin to tug our duffels from the racks.

"Decorum, brothers," Faith Leader says. "Be seated, please. We will unload at the school entrance like the others."

Up there where kids are being let off, boys in heavy coats are hanging out. We inch closer and they look in our direction. Around their necks are wound striped scarves. Like we saw in the brochure, the fronts of their caps are embroidered in gold with the school insignia.

"That's your Welcome Committee," Pastor says. "Think of them as big brothers. They'll get you your new uniforms and show you the ropes. Keep an eye on you."

The bus slides forward, then jerks to a stop. In the playing field next to us, older boys are passing around a cigarette. Jocks in letter jackets laugh, some with their arms draped off each other's shoulders. A tall guy, his cap off, hair chopped in a flattop, shoves a Lower Schooler to the ground. Over by the building's side door, three beefy boys have corralled some dork and are tossing his pack around while the poor kid tries to nab it.

We've been that dork and the boy pushed to the ground. And that kid too, on the baseball diamond, getting hammered by a guy with a red glove on one hand. Just a couple of quick jabs. Boom boom—blood oozes from cut lips and the kid goes down.

In the back of the bus, some of us start blubbering. Others get to praying super fast or rocking back and forth, trying not to wet themselves.

"Gird up now thy loins like a man," Faith Leader says, "for I will demand of thee and answer thou me."

The boy on the baseball diamond boosts himself up, wipes blood and snot from his nose with the fringe of his scarf.

Brother Mullen rises. He crosses the aisle and kneels on an empty seat. He presses his hand against the window. At the end of the street, the sun breaks over the trees. It beams down the length of the bus, lighting up his reddish-blond hair, and the boy on the playing field sees this and lifts his hand too. Minutes pass, both of them silent, their raised hands like antennas.

Faith Leader storms down the aisle and whacks Brother Mullen a good one with a flat hand. The boy crumples onto the seat, a red mark on the side of his face.

Pastor jerks up when he hears this, cranks the hand brake and stands. "Faith Leader Bennett..."

But Taggart, barreling down from the back like a freaking Mack truck, lays Faith Leader out with a single punch. Then Taggart slips in beside Brother Mullen and cups his hand around the tall boy's neck. He snuggles his bald head into Brother Mullen's chest and mumbles something only they can hear.

We don't want to see this. This protectiveness, this deep, wide-open heart. This is not God's plan for us. We have suffered and are now redeemed. We are transformed. Become these gloriously straight butterflies.

We look to Pastor for vindication, but he's hypnotized by those two boys hugging. His face goes all crazy and his shoulders shake. He moans, so long and slow it cuts us deeper than any light saber ever could.

In the aisle, Faith Leader stirs, pushes back onto all fours. He scrambles to his feet and dusts himself off. He scowls at Pastor. "Really? You whimpering about Price again? And in front of the boys? You've lost control, brother. Don't think it's not going in my report."

61

Pastor teeters backward. He reaches for the silver-knobbed handle. He flips the doors open and waves us out.

"Everybody grab their gear and get," Faith Leader says. "Except you two." He knocks Brother Taggart back down the second the Black boy stands. "You two are never fucking getting out."

We snatch our duffels from the racks. As we tromp past Taggart and Mullen, we hawk loogies and spit on them. We call them fudge-packers, faggots, homos, queers. For scripture counsels us that if another believer sins, we must rebuke them.

As we get down from the bus, we pass Pastor Williams. He's collapsed in the driver's seat, slumped over the steering wheel. We used to find his weakness inspiring, but now we see how dangerous it is.

Framed in the open doorway, Faith Leader Bennett flutters his hand above Pastor's shoulder, but he never lets it land. "Leave this behind, brother. It does not profit you anything but Hell."

Pastor straightens, swats Faith Leader's hand away. He doesn't look at him or us or the boy on the playing field trudging to first period. The doors slap shut. The bus squeals and takes off.

We thread our fingers into our belt loops. Hips cocked, glaring straight ahead, we plant ourselves on the sidewalk like our brothers and fathers would, feeling tough and perfectly righteous. Living fucking waters flow within us.

The Welcome Committee marches in our direction. The sun is over their shoulders, so all we see are dark shapes, dark coats, black caps. A gang of boys from the houses we passed, amped for their morning's first fag bash.

A muscle twitches in Brother Stalwart's manly face. He straight-arms his Bible out in front of him, creating a mighty heterosexual force field. "Stand strong in the truth, brothers. For we are one with them now."

The guys in the Welcome Committee say hey. Sweet maple syrup mist rides their breakfast breath. There is a notch in the curve of one chin, a dimple in another. Adam's apples go up and down when they call us brother. When they hug us, through their coats we feel the muscles of their backs. They are like everything solid in the world, those boys.

Our limbs grow heavy. A prickly feeling spreading outward, our insides turned suddenly moist and warm. Then, we shrivel up like a leaf and, like the wind, our sins sweep us away.

Kyle

DARKNESS. Then a dull awareness. A floating sensation of dread. His father's face. Looming out of the void. An angry mask, the human in it warped beyond recognition. His father bellowing, arms raised overhead. THWACK. A red memory of pain spread across Kyle's forehead. Thwack. A fire this time, running along his jaw.

Kyle blinked, then blinked again. In a strobing light, the hood of his old Chevy Vega. A dark lattice of cypress limbs. Below, a net of streetlamps and porch lights. THWACK. No pain. A voice not his father's. Kyle turned his head toward the sound, opened his eyes into a blinding white.

The beam of light jerked away, skittered over the boxes in the backseat. Silhouetted against a red rock cliff, a young woman stood outside his car, rapping on the window. San Francisco Police. Kyle lived in fear of this, each evening switching his sleeping spots.

"License and registration, please," the officer said as Kyle cranked down the window onto a warm October night. Her black uniform hung loosely on her thin frame. A short, curly mat of hair clung to her head like a swim cap. When she shifted her weight to clasp the butt end of the pistol strapped to her duty belt, the glow of a streetlamp lit the contours of her dark face. Kyle could see the mixture of fatigue and vigilance they etched.

"Yes, ma'am," he said, passing her the documents. His father instructed Kyle with his fists, but also by example, to speak deferentially to people up the chain of command. "I went barhopping last night, officer. Thought I better sober up before I drove home. Must've dozed off."

Kyle felt uneasy, starting right off the bat with a falsehood. The Lord detests lying lips, they drilled into him at the Ministry. Every day there, Kyle had to confess his failings, but now he found telling the truth more trouble than it was worth.

In her squad car, the officer radioed in his details, looking smug, Kyle thought, surrounded by the implements and symbols of her authority. Opposite him, the sky was beginning to brighten behind the little natural history museum that perched there on the rocky outcrop above Market Street. Through a gap in some nearby houses, red lights blinked atop Twin Peaks on skeletal Sutro Tower.

The first time Kyle lived in the car was six years earlier. Right after his high school graduation ceremony, he'd thrown his cap and gown in the trash and fled Killeen. The one-story duplex on Fort Hood where he lived with his parents and sister. He still felt guilty about leaving everybody hanging at the little party his mother had planned. About all the burgers and pop she'd bought, the string of gold letters she'd tacked to the wall at the back patio: CONGRATULATIONS, GRAD OF 1981.

He didn't feel sorry one bit on his father's account, though. Kyle's mother told him the man had refused to chase after him, had forbidden her to call the cops. The wages of sin is death, he'd said.

After Kyle split, he drove to Houston in the Chevy, bought with money saved from his gas station job. In Houston, he lied about his age and got hired on for a month as a barback at a gay dive on Montrose. Each night after closing, he slept in the parking lot behind the place in the car. There he had gotten laid, finally, by a man who danced for the Houston Ballet. Kyle thought it was glamorous and daring. He had never been either of those things before.

The officer handed Kyle back his documents. She offered that it looked to be a lovely morning, then told him he better scoot back home.

He was home. His Chevy Vega. This parking lot, nestled between the hill and the row of twisty cypress that hovered above the clamor along the busy street.

HE DROVE HIS CAR out of the museum parking lot and wound down the looping streets. Turning onto Market, he navigated between the rows of two-story commercial buildings, then stashed the car on a side street in the Castro neighborhood. Suit bag draped over one shoulder, he walked to the gym, past Victorians tarted up in bright colors.

In the lightening sky, not even a wisp of the city's signature chilling fog. All summer, horns moaned like lovers coupling in the next room. The sound reassured Kyle he no longer was in landlocked Killeen. Temperatures there often climbed into the hundreds and, though he'd removed the Texan from him, he still missed that heat. Which was why he loved San Francisco best in mid-October, when the sky was clear and the warm air drifted with possibility.

It was a Wednesday, his day at the gym for pecs. He pumped them hard, then showered and shaved with the scanty pre-work crowd. In the locker room mirror, he admired the transformation of Kyle Turner. The paired arcs of a massive chest. The thick neck flaring at the shoulders. The blocky biceps, a prideful vascularity on each, a single bulging blue line. He'd been a scrawny, lonely kid and all this was a mark of belonging. For, if not every gay man in the Castro had a body like his, a great many did or aspired to.

His habit of feeling like an outlier was still strong. And in rebellion from this conventionality, he kept himself clean-shaven and grew his light-auburn hair to his shoulders, where most sported thick mustaches and short crops. Something Kyle hated, as it reminded him of his father and the other enlisted men on Fort Hood.

By 8 a.m., Kyle was dressed in business drag, balancing a paper coffee cup in one hand while jostling in the subway against others similarly attired. Under his arm, he cradled a plastic case containing plans he'd drawn while working at Mark's architecture firm. Kyle had felt bereft when Mark retired and closed up shop. Kyle loved that entry-level job. At lunch in the garden behind the home office on the flanks of Mount Sutro, he listened to Mark's architectural war stories, engrossed by experiences collected over forty years. Kyle's maternal grandfather, C.K. Turner, was a real estate speculator and builder, just as Mark was, and Kyle felt honored to be following in their footsteps.

Before noon, Kyle had interviews at two downtown architecture firms. The men who reviewed his drawings were collegial, but they made no offers. There was always the problem of Kyle's CV. He had only taken a couple of semesters of drafting at community college and had worked at Mark's firm less than three years.

He felt happy after the interviews, even so. Eating his sandwich at a park tucked among the office towers and ringed with lanky, quivering poplars, he felt at one with the throng gathered there, not just by necessity but by the desire to work.

In one corner of the park, a pencil-thin Black man with long, elegant arms carved out a performance space on the grass. He wore a bright-pink dress shirt and a white tie, with earphones clamped to his head, a Walkman hooked at his belt. After a series of balletic turns, he arched backward and did a flip, to the applause of several onlookers.

Kyle fought the old habit of viewing himself unfavorably. He didn't need the Bible verses he memorized at the Ministry to know envy was a sin. Proud as he was of his new body, his muscles now were taut, confining straps. He could no longer reach behind to scratch the middle of his back and he moved with all the grace of a battle tank. Something lost, something gained. He worried that the one canceled out the other.

After lunch, he wandered among the skyscrapers, admiring the architecture, imagining what it would be like to work at one of the big firms there—Gensler, say, or Skidmore, Owings and Merrill—in a drafting room with hundreds of others.

By the time he returned to the Castro, the late afternoon rush hour had begun. The clatter of train cars behind him, he plodded up the Muni subway station's broad steps under a cloudless sky, while around him men discussed their Halloween plans. One had a poodle skirt and a pink angora sweater to die for. Another planned to sashay around the Castro all night wearing nothing but a rhinestone tiara and Doc Martens.

Kyle was carried up Castro Street on this wave of men, past a large poster promoting safe sex—two bare-chested hotties, each with a shiny, square condom package in one hand.

Since he arrived in the city, Kyle was a fixture on that street, a spectacle with his long dark-blond hair touched with ginger. As an antidote for his shyness, he paraded with all the other beauties, posing beside them against the metal picket fence in front of a row of ATMs. Hibernia Beach, after the bank there, was the winking nickname for the place.

"*Hola*, Turner." Behind him, a woman's brazen voice.

He kept walking. Even after three years, sometimes Kyle didn't associate the name *Turner* with himself, only with his grandparents.

"I'm starting to get a complex. You ignoring me?" The voice was close now, ear-splitting, spoken with a Puerto Rican accent, at times so thick he still found it difficult to understand.

In front of the hardware store, Kyle halted suddenly. The guy behind him practically ran him over. Kyle turned and witnessed an onslaught of pedestrians on the sidewalk parting around Rebeca Vasquez, her legs splayed, her hands cupping the waist of her suit jacket. Darkly complected, she had jet-black hair and an inky beauty mark on her right cheek. She was a top real estate agent, a savvy negotiator with a shrewd eye for potential properties. When they met two years earlier at Mark's Christmas party, she was putting together parcels for the firm to develop, afterward selling the completed condo units. Now, she was doing the same for some East Bay guys, but for large commercial projects.

"You did *not* make me come all the way down here," she said. "I've been trolling the street for weeks, looking for your sorry ass."

Ever the salesperson, she was prone to hyperbole. She lived in Dolores Heights, only three blocks away. She and her two lovers frequently banged around here on Castro Street.

"I've been busy."

"With the new Mr What's His Name?"

She seasoned her words with a little singsongy island flavor.

Unlike her, Kyle had blotted out any trace of the way people spoke back home. In Killeen, they ran their words together in a cramped, low growl, as if their jaws had been wired shut. He'd sponged up the speech patterns of every man he tricked with, of the mob of guys in and out of the house farther up Castro Street where he used to live.

"It's not like that. I've been looking for a job."

"You can't pick up the phone? No, wait, don't tell me. You don't have a phone, do you?"

Kyle drew her aside, next to a display of rainbow-colored bath towels in the hardware store window.

"Pac Bell is messing with me," he said, spinning another lie. "You know what pricks the phone company can be."

"Don't bullshit a bullshitter, Turner. I got the whole story from your roommates. Your *former* roommates, I mean."

Just then her demeanor softened. They had been best friends since that Christmas party, dinner and barhopping companions, he her reliable beard and plus-one at business events. They bonded, as well, over their disdain for their difficult religious upbringings. Her family had been swept

74

up by the Evangelical movement overtaking the island and they expected fervor from her every day. Kyle explained that his father returned home from the conflict in Vietnam with a militant religiosity—a lifeline he'd clung to in the prisoner-of-war camps—and punished him and his sister for the slightest lapse. The trauma Kyle suffered at the Ministry, though, he kept to himself.

"Are you in trouble, *mi amor?*" She folded her hand around his wrist.

He hadn't been touched in a week and not even his mother plied him with endearments the way Rebeca did. He was trying to be brave, but with her concern, with the weight and warmth of her hand, hot pinpricks swarmed about his eyes and tears ran down his cheeks.

"Oh, honey," she said. "Let's go get you a doughnut. I know how they cheer you up."

They didn't, really. Lately, a doughnut and a cheap cup of coffee were just all he could afford.

At that time of day, the doughnut shop on Castro Street was nearly empty. In their smudgy glass cases, racks of fried dough beckoned with colorful glazes and speckled toppings. As enticements, large photographs of the same were displayed on the wall. The place was a 24-7 stoners' paradise, a spot to shake off the chill on nights when he went on the prowl.

Rebeca ordered two coffees and they settled into metal chairs at a table next to the window. She screwed up her face when she took her first sip and shoved the paper cup aside. "So, Turner. Give it up."

"I lost my job."

"Remember, I was at Mark's retirement party. That was six months ago, my friend. You must be doing something after that."

"Not really. I picked up some shifts this summer busing tables at my old restaurant, but business was slow."

"How slow, *mi amor?*"

"I couldn't get enough hours to pay my rent."

"You're a little old to be living in a fuck-pad anyway."

"I'm only twenty-four, Rebeca."

"What's that in gay years? Fifty?"

"Funny."

She gave him a toothy smile, cocking her head and placing the tip of a finger just above the beauty mark on her cheek. "I'm a funny girl."

He sipped the burnt coffee. "Well, *Rebequita*. Let me bring you down a bit. I'm living in my fucking car."

"*¡Dios mío!*" Eyes widening, she kissed her fingertips to block any further insensitivity from spilling out of her mouth. "I'm sorry, Kyle honey. I know God is—what you call it?—a sore subject."

He loosened his tie and undid the top button of his dress shirt. "Please don't make me sorry we talked about that. A lot of people had shitty childhoods. Not just us."

"You're not a lot of people, Kyle."

76

"What's that supposed to mean?"

"I care about you, dumb-ass. Come stay with us."

Rebeca was in a ménage with a woman twice her age, an Outward Bound instructor, and another woman, one barely out of diapers, who had recently graduated with a PhD from Stanford Business.

"Thanks, but no. It's pretty crowded at your place."

"Well, how about the new Mr What's His Name?"

"Robert? I don't know. I'd be embarrassed to ask him. He's a big deal in the community."

"Oh?"

"Head of the Bay Area AIDS Coalition."

"Oh." A downward pitch in her voice. She was impressed.

"I feel under-credentialed with his friends. Even when I was working. But telling him I'm homeless? It makes you think of those people lying in doorways at night."

"This is nothing, *mi amor*. It doesn't say anything about you as a person."

Her lilting accent soothed him, as did the open, confident look on her face. His shoulders drifted down as his body relaxed.

She rifled through her purse and retrieved her checkbook. He blocked her, closing the cover with his hand. "*Rebequita*, I'll be fine. I have a place to stay for a couple of nights. I'm pretty sure my mother will spring for some cash. I've got résumés in all over town."

"Can't Mark help you find something?"

"He's got an awful lot on his plate now. A kid. And his new wife, she's a handful."

Rebeca reached across the table and pinched his cheek. "Well, let *mami* work her Rolodex. Those dickhead clients of mine have got to be good for something besides making cash, no?" She pulled a tissue from her purse and dabbed her eyes with it. "Oh, you are so spoiling my hard-ass reputation here, *mi amor*."

"I'm really sorry I didn't call. I guess I felt ashamed."

"Pride goeth before a fall, young man."

"Proverbs 16:18, yes."

A BANK OF PAY PHONES lined one side of Hibernia Beach and Kyle slipped into a booth and placed a call. Nearing the crest of Twin Peaks, the sun blasted through the glass, making it too warm inside to louver the doors shut. He hung his sports coat on a handle, then curled his hand around the transmitter when his mother's voice said, yes, she would accept the charge.

His mother had been devastated over having caved to her husband's demand they cure their gay son. Ever since, she was Kyle's chief ally and confidante. Each Wednesday, like this, he phoned her at five o'clock over at her friend Myrtle's. Kyle's father worked a flex schedule as a flight instructor at Fort Hood and Kyle didn't want to risk calling home on the chance that he might pick up.

"I can't stand it another minute, Kyle." Her Texas twang chirped in the receiver like steel cables scissoring in the wind. "Your father, this god-awful place."

"That new house of yours is nice, isn't it?"

"It's fine, I guess. Look, I may be the world's slowest learner, but after twenty-five years I finally got the memo: I am *not* cut out to be an army wife."

"Mom, it's just not a good time for you to come out here." As he spoke, he wound and unwound the spiral phone cord around his index finger.

"I tell you what, we ought to both go back to Dallas. Your grandfather is semiretired now, but one of his partners would surely take you on. Have you ever thought about selling real estate?"

"Mom, I've got this. Please." His voice sounded whiny, as if he was twelve again.

"It's a perfectly good plan. That big house of theirs is practically empty. You love the pool."

"Why don't you stay with them for a while, Mom? When I'm back on my feet, I'll find you a nice place nearby."

On the sidewalk, the after-work crowd was thinning. Laughter gusted through the open storefront of a restaurant across the street. Inside the darkened room, above a crowd of early diners, little halogen lamps floated on cables and cast a reddish light. It felt womblike, the sheltering interior, another place he was too broke to enter. He wasn't

79

accustomed to displays of emotion. Even when he was depressed, he tended to drift in a clouded absence of sensation. But on the tailwinds of Rebeca's nurturing, hearing his mother's desperation, the chatty people in the restaurant having fun, for the second time that day his eyes welled with tears.

"Mom, you understand why I can't go back to Texas, don't you?"

A barely perceivable hiss played across the line.

"You still live in that apartment with all those boys? I'm mean, they're a hoot and everything, especially that Lance fellow."

"Luke, Mom."

"Well, there were just so many of them and the place, if you'll excuse me, is a little tawdry. You can do better, son."

"I don't live there anymore, Mom. I moved in with a friend—this great house up the hill. Fabulous views."

More lies. She would work herself into a state, though, if he admitted he was homeless.

"I don't know, Kyle. My parents have their problems, but they've stuck it out over forty years. If I abandoned your father now, they'd never let me hear the end of it."

"Really? Seemed to me they were never all that crazy about Dad."

"It's the principle, son. Married people of their generation aren't required to be happy."

"How's Rachel?"

80

"You hate your sister."

"I'm just asking."

"Fine. It's her senior year at UT Austin. She's treasurer of her sorority, if you can believe that. I thought they would have kicked her out by now. And for some reason, she gave up math."

"Oh?"

"Switched her major to accounting. Already working for some cheerleading supply company down there. She's got the whole outfit now. Pom-poms and everything. I've never understood that girl. Always so impetuous. Not like my sweet, dependable Kyle."

"You know I want you to come, don't you?" he said.

"You should call your grandfather. He misses you."

"I'll try. And Mom?"

"Yes?"

"Can you send me some money?"

"Call your grandfather."

AFTER HE HUNG UP with his mother, Kyle grabbed a bag of peanuts and a bottle of orange juice at a corner store. He headed to the car and made his way back to the natural history museum. The sky darkening over Twin Peaks was mirrored in its windows. The parking lot emptied, the little museum was freed now of chattering children. There was only the whisper of cypress needles in the warm breeze, the occasional raucous call of a Steller's jay.

Kyle couldn't beg for more money and confess his recent failures to his grandfather. The old man had already done enough. Besides, they hadn't spoken since the graduation ceremony. They had been close once, and though Kyle hadn't excelled at school, his grandfather had been especially proud. His mother fretted, but understood why Kyle had run off. In contrast, his grandfather had taken it hard. What explanation could Kyle give, if he were to contact the old man, for trading his beloved Texas for iniquitous San Francisco? Not the truth, certainly.

A police siren bellowed below; red-and-blue lights zipped across the building facades along Market Street. He tensed reflexively. He took a chance coming back here, but everywhere he parked was dicey. Of all his sleeping spots, this floating perch above the Castro was the best. He even visited here nights back when he was working, whenever he was depressed, just to sit on the bench behind the museum and stare off into the city lights.

"Oh man, greatly loved," Kyle said to himself, "fear not, peace will be with you."

At the Ministry they studied the Bible night and day, a kind of twisted alchemy meant to transform gay into straight. The result had been his contorted thoughts. Countering these were the Bible passages on peace and love, on compassion for others and the life of the spirit. He felt the presence of these qualities in that little parking lot with the light dimming and the stars winking on.

He popped a handful of peanuts in his mouth and washed them down with the juice. He threaded his tie from his collar and draped it across the plan case resting on the dash. Unbuttoning his dress shirt, he tugged the tails from his chinos and shrugged the shirt off. All this was executed in what had become a kind of military precision. He didn't love the occasional run-ins with the cops. But after three months of living on the street, he felt like a warrior—with the resourcefulness it required—not in a way his father could appreciate, but a warrior just the same.

Streetlamps tinged the interior of the car a cold blue. From the plan case, he popped grayed vellum sheets and rolled them out on the passenger seat. In the title block: KYLE TURNER. Mullen, no more. Four hundred dollars and a quick signature had blotted out the last vestige of his father.

The house plans were so thin in places as to be nearly translucent, worn by an electric eraser where he had repeatedly altered them. He had been close to finishing when Mark retired and closed the office.

Something about the lover's studio didn't feel right, tucked as it was against the sharp angle of the hill. From the glove compartment Kyle pulled out his leather notebook. It fell open at the cloth marker on a pencil sketch of a sleeping Robert, his new—what?—boyfriend?

The portrait was densely shaded within the straight margins he'd ruled onto the page. Kyle had struggled to get the hooded eyes right, their web of wrinkles sprouting at each corner, the closely trimmed gray beard. And, too, the man's ever-present hint of a smile. Even asleep, Robert's face gave off that pleasant impression that Kyle found so hard to penetrate.

He flipped to a fresh page, looped the cloth marker over the top of the journal. *Lover's studio needs more light,* he scratched in blue ink with his fountain pen. Sometimes he imagined the man working there might be Robert, saving the world from AIDS. Other times, he was an artist. Or his first lover even, Cecil Taggart, who Kyle met at the Ministry. Given the circumstances, the relationship had been difficult to consummate. Before they found a way, Brother Taggart, as they called him, ran away.

Cecil talked about San Francisco as if it was the Promised Land. When Kyle arrived in the city, it saddened him not to find Cecil there. Maybe he was one of the ones who didn't thrive—suicides, drug overdoses, years secreted in loveless marriages, turning tricks nights at highway rest stops.

KYLE LEFT HIS CAR at the museum and descended the two flights of stairs to Market Street, his suit bag hook digging into the bend of one finger. When he reached the motel, he peered into the brightly lit but unattended office. Through a partially opened door, blue light flickered in the back room. He pressed the button on the metal frame and the front door buzzed, then clicked open. In the back room, he found Sammy sprawled on a beat-up leather sofa, mashing a red button on the joystick in his lap. On a black-and-white computer screen, crude figures jerked through a brick maze to the sound of gunfire, Nazi soldiers barking orders.

The young man was dressed in a shiny black T-shirt and meticulously ripped jeans. A small silver ring pierced one nostril. Almost imperceptibly, his eyes scanned Kyle, a look that meshed lust with geeky admiration.

In his tight jeans and tank top, Kyle felt exposed, embarrassed, then a familiar heat, a wave outward from his groin. "Hey," he shouted over the noise coming from the computer.

"Keys on the desk. Fresh towels and soap are already up there." Sammy torqued the joystick and grimaced, slid his tongue out the side of his mouth. "I was beginning to think I wasn't getting another chance. That you'd found a job or something."

"No such luck."

From the computer, static and a crashing sound, blocky letters on the screen: YOU HAVE BEEN KILLED. Sammy tossed the joystick aside. "Can you believe this? Shit's so old. My uncle's one cheap-ass motherfucker." Kyle had seen Sammy's uncle around the place. A man with a long, arrogant mustache kept meticulously waxed, he was the most recent in a long line of Pakistani owners of the motel.

Sammy bobbed his head as if he was grooving to the synth-pop music he liked. He took in Kyle again, eyes widening in his dark face. "Well, good luck for me, then.

Number eight. You know the drill. Don't mess up anything. Everything but the bathroom's been cleaned."

KYLE WAS BASKING under the water's sharp, hot spray—a luxury, this second shower of the day—when he heard a knock. Dripping wet, one towel wrapped around his waist, another slung over his shoulder, Kyle hurried to the door. He opened it to find Sammy peering over the rail down to the darkened office, a bedspread cradled in one arm.

Turning to Kyle, he grinned and shut the door behind him. He flung the bedspread into the air. When it settled, he smoothed it out on the floor and sat cross-legged, his small frame accomplishing all this in a series of quick, self-contained moves.

Kyle slipped the towel off his shoulder and rubbed it across his long hair. "How was the tour?" Improbably, or so Kyle thought, the classically trained Sammy was the bassist in a thrash metal band.

"Our guitar player ran off with some chick in Sacramento. My uncle had to return all the advances the venues paid us, which, of course, we'd already spent." Sammy slowly tugged the corner of the towel around Kyle's waist. It arched open like a theater curtain and puddled at Kyle's feet.

Returning to the bathroom, Kyle knocked his tooth-brush against the rim of the sink and packed it back in its case. "You said your uncle was cheap."

"Not if he thinks it'll give him some leverage."

Kyle snapped off the lid of the deodorant stick. "There are other jobs."

"What, like making copies for seven bucks an hour? Or shoveling shit at Burger Fucking King? Hell, no. Besides, you don't understand our family. Nobody gets out alive."

Kyle returned to the bedroom and settled on the coverlet opposite Sammy.

"We going to just chat again this time?" Sammy said.

"Sorry. Today was cool, but it's not like I get to talk to people all that much."

With his hand, Sammy lightly traced the inside of Kyle's thigh. "You know, I could say the same about you. There are other jobs."

Kyle stretched out on his side, propped his head on one angled arm. "It's a profession, Sammy. You don't just walk away from it."

Sammy shook his head slightly. "I don't get it. Can't you use the good-looking-gay-boy network or something to find another architecture job?"

Kyle worried the folds of the bedspread, the flower pattern bunching under his fingertips. "I didn't go to college."

"I guess you would need a degree for that."

"Just a bachelor's. If you have good drafting skills, like I do, you can work without it, but it's harder."

"It's not hard now." Sammy squeezed Kyle's cock in his hand.

"I'm tired, Sammy."

The young man laughed, but minimally, as if that tiny gesture would conceal how he felt. It tumbled out anyway as he withdrew his hand. "You wouldn't be with me if you had any money."

"Why do you say things like that?"

"You muscly white boys only hang with each other."

Kyle still felt weird being described like that, but prideful as well. After the long abstinence of his teenage years, it thrilled him that most of his interactions here in the city were based around sex—even during the most mundane of activities: folding T-shirts at the laundromat while being cruised by some hunk, trolling supermarket aisles and pretending to shop for detergent. But the hierarchies from which he benefited—race, beauty, manliness—troubled him now. They seemed another kind of lie. He wasn't the sexual athlete he appeared to be, the star always looking to score with some other A-lister. He had to acknowledge that his tastes, when it came to men, were broader than his idea of them. They were unpredictable.

He lifted the hem of Sammy's T-shirt, Kyle's fatigue powerless to dampen the excitement he felt when the white cloth revealed the man's slender body. When Sammy's erection snapped against his taut stomach as he wriggled out of his underwear.

Pressing into Sammy, feeling his heat, the smoothness of his skin, was for Kyle, after so many days alone, an almost unbearable relief. For a moment during sex, just before Kyle lost the ability to observe himself, he gazed into Sammy's eyes and felt an electric connection to the man that urged him on to climax, and that felt deeply right.

Once spent, Kyle slid across Sammy's sweat-slicked body onto the floor and lay on his back. He peeled the condom off and wadded it into a tissue. Pillowing his head on his forearm, he listened to the slowing of Sammy's breath.

At the Ministry, they'd instilled in Kyle a hatred of the body, drilling the message with chapter and verse. He felt it again creep over him. Staring at the ceiling that now seemed miles away, his thoughts and feelings were muddied by the panic welling inside him over having just then done something terribly wrong.

"I was thinking, maybe I could sleep here tonight." Sammy pushed up against Kyle and leaned in to kiss him.

Tugging the edge of the bedspread over his naked body, Kyle rolled onto his side, away from the man. "Not tonight."

"You know what? Fuck you." Sammy leapt off the floor and stumbled back into his clothes while he talked. "My boyfriend thinks you're a walking billboard for everything that's wrong with America: an obsession with surfaces, with size. He doesn't understand my fascination with you."

"You told him about us?" Kyle rolled onto his back and the bedspread slipped down to the broad, swooping arc of his chest.

"In all its gruesome detail. He says sex with you sounds like a military invasion. That you fuck too hard."

"Looked like you were enjoying it to me."

"Yeah, well, it doesn't mean he's not right."

"Come on, now. You know I like you; think I made that pretty obvious. It's just...I'm living on the street, Sammy. I need to get a good night's sleep for once and not worry about being hassled by the cops."

Sammy paused at the door, his hand on the knob. "When do you want your wake-up call, asshole?"

"Sammy, don't be like that."

"The call."

"Four thirty."

"You got an early interview?" Sammy eyed the suit bag laid out on the bed.

"Something like that."

Sammy slumped against the open door, behind him lights on the other side of the courtyard and shining pinpricks in the cloudless sky. "Maybe tomorrow night we can sleep together."

"Definitely."

"Well then, leave everything like you found it. Okay?"

KYLE'S CAR GLIDED to a stop between the cones of light cast by two lampposts. The motor cut, quiet returned to the street, but backgrounded by the always-present grumbling of the city. The amorphous bulks of wood-framed houses faced off against each other in the dark, the roofs to the east hard-lined against the brightening sky. Just ahead, above Mount Sutro's shadowed flanks, the tower blinked its red warning.

Kyle shimmied tight the knot of his tie, straightened the shirt collar. Mixing with the scent of the eucalyptus trees on Mount Sutro, the sweet smell of Sammy's cologne drifted from Kyle's fingertips.

Dark windows gaped from the top two floors of the house. On its stucco wall, their firm's small plaque, recently removed, left a ghostly trace. At the side door, his plan case wedged under one arm, a penlight held butt end in his mouth, Kyle punched the combination into the lock.

Carefully, he pulled the door shut. The flashlight's beam slid across the project photos that punctuated a broad brick wall—condos, townhomes, single-family houses. It crept across the half-empty bookshelves of Sweet's catalogs and code books, across the cardboard boxes strewn haphazardly on the glossy wooden floor. A diffuse light filtered in from the garden through broad windows.

He draped his sports coat off the back of the padded office chair, flicked on the drafting lamp and slid the vellum sheets from the tube. He taped the corners of the ground-floor plan to his drafting table's green plastic cover.

In his mind, he stood in the bedroom of his dream house, the shower burbling behind the bathroom door. Robert sang in his lovely tenor. Then it was Cecil Taggart, the boy from the Ministry, talking on the phone in his studio in his rich East Texas–inflected bass. Kyle realized it wasn't the studio that needed revision but the dining room, too small for entertaining. With electric eraser, triangle and pencil, he expanded the room, contracted another, punched openings in the building's elevation. He was thrilled to be moving toward perfection, feeling ever closer to the life he was to share there with the man he loved.

Noises from the living quarters upstairs. He checked his watch; he'd lost track of time. He'd need to hurry and finish up if he was to avoid running into Mark's new wife.

He froze when he heard the door open at the top of the stairs. The overhead fluorescent lights stuttered on. Two small oxford shoes appeared in the triangle where the stairs' open stringer met the low ceiling. The little girl's face filled it for a second, then disappeared.

"Mommy, somebody's down here," she said in her perfect American accent.

More footsteps, urgently drumming the tile floor upstairs, advancing to the top landing.

"Go back to the kitchen now, Sherry." The voice of Mark's wife, shrill, always hectoring.

She burst down the stairs, her intricately patterned running shoes slapping the bare wooden treads. Sheathed head to toe in tight black spandex, she halted at the bottom landing, her legs slightly bent. Eyes open wide, her brow knit and her cheeks puffed out, she brandished a rolling pin overhead, whose handle almost scraped the low tile ceiling. Kyle stifled a laugh. She looked to him like some deranged, black-clad ninja, some overly expressed comic book character.

"Kyle?" She lowered the rolling pin. Under a sweatband that carved a yellow swath across her smart, short cut, the look on her face now was one of disapproval. "You frightened me. We weren't expecting you." She spoke with a British accent, slightly inflected by her Hong Kong Chinese.

"I left a message last night."

"We got back late from the movies. Haven't checked them yet."

"I'm sorry to cause a fuss."

"Look, I know you and my husband have this arrangement. But the next time, please wait until one of us confirms the date."

"Yes, ma'am." It seemed ridiculous treating her with deference. She was barely older than he was.

"Besides, we're getting rid of all this in two weeks." She waved a hand across the contents of the room, while twiddling her fingers dismissively. "As you know, my husband is no longer required to work. He does, however, need to shed a few pounds. We're converting the space into an exercise room."

The little girl slunk down the stairs to slump against her mother's leg. She wore a plaid wool skirt, a navy-blue jacket over a white dress shirt and striped tie. She stuck out her tongue at Kyle and grinned. He liked the girl, thought she was smart. When he worked there with Mark, he made her laugh by talking silly with a mash of lunch in his mouth.

Slippered feet followed the rise and run of the steps. Mark, dressed in a white bathrobe, a red *W* embroidered on its chest, positioned himself behind his new daughter. He settled his hands on the girl's shoulders, forming, along with his young wife, a so-perfect family vignette.

"What's with the rolling pin, dear?"

"I was defending the house. We had an intruder. Sherry, come on. Breakfast. School."

The girl scrunched up her nose and stuck out her tongue again at Kyle. She trudged behind her mother, who had wheeled around and was taking the steps by twos.

It was true, since the woman arrived, Kyle frequently felt the intruder in the house. Those few times, back when the firm was open, when he fetched something upstairs for Mark, her icy presence made him feel unwelcomed. In Mark's bachelor days, he frequently invited Kyle upstairs, he and the senior draftsman, a lanky, goateed graduate from UC Berkeley. They'd drink beer, have Thai food delivered. They'd argue over the latest 49ers game or critique the new buildings downtown—Philip Johnson's faceted tower at the foot of California Street, the stacked vertical planes of Four Embarcadero nearby.

"I did call last night," Kyle said. "I left a message."

"It's really my fault. I checked the answering machine when we came in. Sherry, though, insists I read her stories for an hour after my wife gets her ready for bed. With all that, last night your message slipped my mind."

Mark scanned the room: the three drafting stations, the small conference table by the windows, the kitchenette. "We did some good work in this place. Apparently, though, I'm about to get fit." Mark shot Kyle a dopey smile and shrugged his shoulders. "Listen, I was about to have coffee. Will you join me?"

"Sure, I'd like that."

"Meet you in the garden in ten."

Kyle untaped the vellum sheet, threaded it, along with the others, into the tube and joggled on the top. He looped his jacket over one forearm. The garden through the large windows had now come fully into view. Past an arrangement of redwood deck furniture swayed a bank of hostas, their broad leaves yellowing, their fruiting stalks arched under the weight of the seedpods.

Kyle pushed through the drafting room door onto the deck as Mark descended the exterior wooden stairs from the main floor. He had changed into a light ribbed sweater and baggy khaki pants, and was carrying a coffee mug in each hand. His gray hair had grown shaggy since Kyle last saw him and his round face was stubbled with the beginnings of a beard.

Mark arranged the mugs on a low table of frosted glass and took a seat next to it in a cushioned deck chair. "Splash of half-and-half, no sugar. Right?"

"Right."

Kyle grabbed the mug nearest him, planted one end of the case on the deck, leaning against the tube as if it were a cane. "Sorry for all the confusion."

"Don't be. I'm glad for the chance to catch up. I've been meaning to call you, but…" Mark gestured to the house behind him with one hand, then pointed to Kyle's plan case. "I guess they won't let you do outside work on your new job. Some firms are picky about that."

Concealing his look of indecision behind his coffee mug, Kyle mulled over what to say—a plausible half-truth, something face-saving. "I haven't found a job yet, actually," he said, finally. "What I mean is…I'm still trying to find the right fit."

"Oh?" Mark said with an air of concern. "I just assumed you were coming here before your new job, because of your business clothes."

Kyle lowered his head. There was birdsong under the brightening sky and people chattering through the open windows of the houses nearby. Another in a string of fine October mornings. He considered telling Mark an outright lie: a job interview before lunch, a second that afternoon. Kyle had fibbed to him before, of course, to keep from revealing the details of his slutty weekends, his sexed-up holiday trips. You couldn't let straight people in on that kind of thing. But he'd never lied to Mark about anything important and he wasn't going to start.

"It makes me feel better, on weekdays, to dress for work. To pretend I have someplace to go."

"I see." The tone of Mark's voice floated upward, so that this sounded more like a question.

A commotion through an open window of the house. Upstairs, the girl threw back the curtains and watched them while she ate from a yogurt cup. Behind her, Mark's wife spoke Cantonese into a phone, motioning broadly with her hands in their direction.

"Sit, won't you," Mark said, indicating the chair opposite him. "You're making me nervous. I'm trying to get a hold on that."

Kyle leaned the case against the glass table and sat.

"Those plans you're working on, what are they, then? I've been meaning to ask."

Kyle gripped the handle of his mug tighter. "It's a house. Single-family. But it's not a real project. Not yet, anyway. It's speculative."

"A spec house? For a builder? Great. Which one?"

"I guess *speculative*'s not the right word. It's more of a dream house for me and, well, my significant other."

"You've met someone. Excellent. What's the lucky man's name?"

"I don't know. Robert, maybe?"

Furrows etched Mark's brow, followed by a slackening of his face. "You know you can come to me, Kyle. If you're … If you have any concerns. Anything at all."

"I don't know."

"You don't know what?"

"I guess…well, it's hard. I never expect people to be there for me."

Mark tapped his wedding ring against the ceramic cup, the percussive sound quiet yet oddly piercing. "How old are you? Twenty-one? Twenty-two?"

"Twenty-four."

"I started in this business same as you. Young. Only a little community college. I'd worked construction, though, every summer in high school. When I struck out on my own, I was one cocky son of a gun. Like you, eager to get going. An ignorant little shit, but lucky. Dad's money, plus I hired some guys twice my age who could design and build houses with blindfolds on. Do you understand?"

"Yeah, I guess so."

"I don't think you do. I don't think any of us do. What I'm getting at is, after forty years of sweat and toil, some hardship, a little success, as you know, I'm still counting on other people to save my ass."

Mark glanced over his shoulder at his young wife. She was glaring down at them through the window, her arms crossed at her chest. "There are days when I fear I haven't found the appropriate vessel. Or that this dependence reveals a weakness of character."

"And other days?"

"It seems like God's plan. Or Buddha's. Something. I don't know."

A breeze drifted in from the ocean. High up, from the twisting skeins, came a croaking of sandhill cranes.

"She and I will travel, I guess. That last project of ours really put a crimp in the honeymoon. The plan is to show me off to the Hong Kong relatives who couldn't make the wedding, then take a cruise around the world. She did that her gap year, apparently. Loved it. Hard proposition to pass up, given her father's paying for everything."

Mark swirled the last of the coffee in the mug and tossed it back. "What I'd like to do is show her America. New York and San Francisco, I keep telling her, they aren't the real America. I'd like us to go to some of those places I never got around to seeing when I was young. But I'll happily embrace the foreign. We put ourselves into a position and we do the best we can."

Kyle slid a fingertip down the rib of the plan case. He'd poured himself into those drawings. He saw, though, that they would never be completed. That house existed solely as dream. How pitiful, he thought. Real buildings transformed the ordinary—how people lived, how they felt, how they breathed and fucked.

Kyle crumpled against the cushion of the chair. "Do we need to do anything? Can we, even?"

It was an odd thing to say, Kyle knew, but Mark laughed.

"Perhaps not," Mark said. "Still, we aren't men who thrive on idleness, you and I. Are we, Kyle Turner?"

For the third time in twenty-four hours, Kyle fought back tears. He made a brave attempt to match Mark's laugh, for he was grateful that this man he so admired would draw the comparison. "No, sir. It appears we are not."

On the first floor of the house came the whoosh of the seal breaking around the door.

"Mark, I'm walking Sherry to school now, then off for a quick run. Be ready when I get back. Remember, we're meeting my cousins at the Legion of Honor for lunch and the Rodin after. You and your little friend need to finish up."

Mark's wife closed the door with a thump and strode off.

"I don't think she likes me very much," Kyle said.

"For all the privileges she's had, she's actually led a very sheltered life. She doesn't like what she doesn't understand. She finds you unusual."

Kyle winced. "Is that what you think too?"

"I think you've lost your way, is all. They tell me it's easy to find. That first we must just relax."

Into Kyle's memory flashed more words from the New Testament: Do not let yourselves be troubled, but believe. For faith, it is the assurance of things hoped for, the conviction of things not yet seen. It annoyed Kyle how these simplistic injunctions still intruded on his thinking. He attempted to push them away, along with the images of his time at the Ministry, but they would never relent.

But in the scripture's wake came a new understanding—clear now, where it had only nagged at him around the edges before. What he had to do.

"When are you off on your trip?" Kyle said.

"Nothing's set. Sherry has school. Next summer, maybe. Why?"

"Before you go, I'd like for you to show me how buildings work. I mean really, not just on paper. Help me study for the licensing exams too. Help me become an architect. Like you."

"That's my boy." Mark blushed, revealing his embarrassment, Kyle sensed, over voicing this endearment so directly. Mark rose to his feet and extended his hand. "We can start tomorrow, if you'd like."

Kyle stood, grasping it, shaking it vigorously. "Yes, sir. I would. I'd like that very much."

Robert

IT WAS the beginning of June and the San Francisco fog machine was going full tilt. Five o'clock the previous evening, right on schedule, it slumped over the rim of Twin Peaks like clammy cotton batting and blanketed the city. In the morning, as I drank my latte at our marble breakfast bar, I watched it retreat under the sun's onslaught, comforted by the cycle's predictability. Little else was in those days.

Case in point: Kyle.

He occupied the doorway set into the row of picture windows that looked out onto the deck. The sun, lifting off over the Oakland Hills across the bay, tucked under the morning's gray remnants and set his long auburn hair aflame. Even after five years together, I never tired of ogling him. His tall, heavily muscled body was obscured in silhouette, but his handsome face came through the shadow. The perfectly straight nose, the high cheekbones, the angular jaw with its cleft chin.

He eyed my Domobar Super—the dual-boiler, polished stainless steel espresso machine—as though its arms and dials might suddenly spring to life and beat the crap out of him. "Robert, honey?"

"Let me guess," I said, "your mother would like more coffee."

Case in point Number Two: the inimitable Diane, who for eight months had been living downstairs from us in the aptly named mother-in-law apartment.

"Could you please? That thing scares the heck out of me."

Since his mother's relocation from Texas, Kyle's speech had synchronized with her clipped twang. He skimped on the details when outlining his unhappy childhood, the difficulties with his father. His mother was equally tight-lipped. So, his new country-inflected affectation helped me to feel connected, even if on a superficial level, to that unspoken part of his past.

The Domobar's complexity was not his only reason for disliking the machine. It was an expensive gift from my previous boyfriend, a hedge fund manager at Schwab. Kyle was threatened by the man's occasional phone calls asking me to hook up. I declined his invitations, though sometimes too reluctantly, which would set Kyle to banging doors shut and sulking around the house.

Any other person in his position would parlay that country bumpkin charm, beauty and youth into getting what he wanted, but Kyle suffered from a bad case of over-earnestness. He pressed his hand to my chest. "Honey, I know. She's a lot."

Under his soulful gaze, how could I not relent? Minutes later, I carried a tray of lattes out onto the deck, extra foamy for Diane, who preferred her coffee fluffy, with just a hint of a tan. She was enthroned on the wicker sofa next to her son. By the time I came on the scene, she had been to the city many times yet persisted in dyeing her red hair an unnatural black and wearing pantsuits that could only pass for chic in the small Texas town she was from. I packed her off to a stylist, who gave her pencil-thin brows, stripped her hair of color and cropped it at the sides. The front he upswept in a rusty tsunami with its crest of white. Then, they went clothes shopping. That morning, she sported a flamingo-pink sweater and black stiletto pants that showed off her trim figure. A strand of pearls lapped an embroidered floral top.

I set the tray in front of her on the low table.

"Oh, how terribly sweet of you, son."

Lately she'd been calling me this, with a veneer of gentility that felt simultaneously complimentary and threatening.

I sat next to Kyle in the adjoining deck chair and drank my latte while they chatted about their plans. Under a troupe of glaucous-winged gulls drifting in the thinning mists, the pace of the city below was proceeding full throttle. Cars whizzed along Market Street; at its intersection with Castro, poles of electric buses rattled through the clutter of overhead cables.

It was a Friday, nearly 10 a.m. We were dawdling. I'd phoned my assistant, Sharon, to say I was coming in late to the office. And Kyle's boss, an Oakland builder, had given Kyle the day off to make up for the overtime he put in on the Memorial Day weekend.

"I wish I could join you," I said. "It'll be gorgeous up there once the fog burns completely off." They were driving my Audi on a trip across the bay up Mount Tamalpais.

When I laced Kyle's fingers through mine, Diane stiffened. I wasn't sure why my displays of affection with her son made her uncomfortable. Not the gay thing—she bragged on the phone to her friend in Texas about her glorious new situation. Maybe it was a residue from her prudish life on the army base where she and her husband had been stationed.

She ought to have been impressed her son was partnered with the director of a large AIDS organization, but a steady diet of perky morning talk shows limited her awareness of the calamity. Probably, I was too ancient, two years older than she. Fifty-two to Kyle's twenty-eight. And quite likely, she simply believed no one could ever be good enough for her boy.

I slid the last bit of foam into my mouth and returned my cup to the tray. "I was wondering how the apartment hunt is going."

Kyle and his mother turned to each other and screwed up their faces, like girls on a park bench who'd been flashed by some old man.

"Just to remind you," I said, "my sister and her husband are visiting middle of September. Thinking we'd have this all taken care of, I promised them the downstairs apartment."

"Robert, we've just been so busy," Diane said in a twang more pronounced than her son's. She wet a finger on her tongue, then attempted to wipe off the lipstick smudge on the lip of her cup. "And the middle of September. That's just so far off, isn't it? I mean, how hard could it be to find some place around here?"

"In three and a half months?" I said. "Very. It's San Francisco, Diane. Everybody and their mother wants to live here. Obviously." I opened my hand, palm up, in their direction.

"Well, you know," she said, "Kyle and I have been away from each other so long. He wants to show me every little thing. Northern California. And those hidden places in the city. God, all those stairs! The Filbert steps. The Lyon. What's that one around here?"

"Monument Way?" Kyle said. "Mount Olympus?"

"I don't know. It's just all so lovely—nothing like Texas—but, Robert, I tell you what, it wears me completely out."

"Look, Diane," I said, beginning to feel put upon. "You've been here nearly a year now."

"I know." She gazed beamingly back at her son. "The most glorious year of my life."

✦ ✦ ✦

I SPRANG UP the steps by twos to our new second-floor offices above Market Street, driven by my continued annoyance with Diane. Another three weeks of inaction on the apartment front had led me to pop off to her that morning. She batted her eyes and started in on another aw-shucks routine, telling me: Let's not get into all that just now, Robert darlin'. She was still on a high from the parade yesterday.

It was her first Gay Pride and she got all decked out in a rainbow-colored blouse and matching sun hat. She hooted and hollered—louder than anyone lined up nearby along Market Street—at each passing float of virtually naked musclemen in leather short-shorts or drag queens with hair as high as the Transamerica Pyramid.

During our row that morning, the way Diane looked at me as I explained, yet again, how little time there was before my sister and her husband came, I got the impression she thought their visit a ruse to evict her.

Not a ruse, exactly, just a blessed coincidence. Excited as I was by the upcoming visit, the main reason I wanted Diane out was that she put a crimp in my and Kyle's sex life. He always slunk off into the hinterlands of our big king-size bed when my erection and I nuzzled up to him, fearing his mother three stories below would hear our groans and ass slaps.

When I reached the top of the office stairs, I stopped for a moment to admire the trim modernist lettering beneath the rainbow bunting: *Bay Area* AIDS *Coalition*. I slowed my breathing and pushed through the door.

"Surprise!"

The entire staff and quite a few volunteers were assembled in reception, waving their arms and grinning. A banner was suspended overhead.

CONGRATS, CAPTAIN STOLLAR
FIVE YEARS AT THE HELM!

I was mobbed by people—shaking hands, patting me on the back. All wore identical white T-shirts, the name of the organization screened on the back. On the front: CAPTAIN STOLLAR, in big Helvetica bold. And below, my face superimposed on Cary Grant's crisply uniformed frame— as B.F. Pinkerton in *Madame Butterfly*.

"Sharon?" I said to my assistant, the squat lesbian with the beaming red face, whom I knew to be an old-movie buff. "This is you, isn't it?" I pointed to the T-shirt.

If it were possible, she beamed even wider, then placed me in a hug that nearly squeezed the breath out of me.

When she let go, she handed me one of the shirts and insisted I slip it over my Izod.

That she'd misidentified Pinkerton's rank should have been endearing, but her usual lack of attention to detail annoyed me. There wasn't room here for error. People's lives depended on us. I'd fire her, but she was popular with staff. Also, it might send the wrong signal to the women's community, who by that point had become our chief ally.

"Speech. Speech," a group of volunteers called from over in one corner.

The room quieted. I said what one says. It wasn't about me, but them. About the young man at hospice surrounded by caregivers, his new friends. About the families, out-of-towners given temporary housing to be at their sons' bedsides at SF General. About the brave men and women at Visiting Nurses doing thankless work. About everyone we'd helped. Everyone we'd lost.

Someone rang a meditation bell and we bowed our heads.

I closed the door to my office and tried to collect myself. These pep talks were necessary—the work frequently grim, the outcomes rarely good—but they took a toll. Thirty years in public health hadn't prepared me for this challenge. We and our partners created nearly everything from scratch: care buddy teams, integrated home health systems, end-of-life assistance. Advocacy for compassionate release of the too few new treatments. Not in the streets like ACT

UP, whose work we supported, but at city hall, in committee rooms in Sacramento and DC.

None of this had been suggested by my upbringing. My father, a stuff-shirt Bostonian, was—like Kyle's mentor, Mark—a successful residential architect. From an early age, he insisted I accompany him to his studio, where he made me spend long hours tinkering with wooden blocks, cooking up spaces and cutting and gluing models of them out of thin gray board. The focus on objects depressed me. From that awareness sprang my desire to reform, not a visual, tactile world, but broken bodies. Families on the edge. People dying or in grief.

I even came to understand the connection between this desiring to do good and the whirlwind sexual activity I engaged in when I first got to the city. The same body that grew ill and wasted away, also needed. Also lusted.

I'd tried to get Kyle on board with that, urging him to reconnect with the sexual exuberance of our tribe. Saturday, the two of us would separate to discover what the night had in store. Even with my average looks and so-so body, it was easy to get laid. Epidemic or no, none of those men lined up outside the bar after last call wanted to make the trip home alone.

On nights when I had use of our house, I'd rush back with a new playmate in tow, only to find Kyle flat out on the couch in the living room, splayed on his chest a thick manual on structural engineering or HVAC systems that Mark had given him. Often, he would be freakishly gaping at the ceiling, seemingly unaware of our presence as the man and I slunk by him on the way to the bedroom at the top floor.

That Kyle was a homebody now made sense. After losing his previous job, the months of homelessness until I took him in. Before that, the slingshotting between apartments of hard-partying young gay men—the drugs, the sex—which was all shits and giggles when he arrived in the city, but alienating finally.

But this blank state I so often found him in concealed something deeper. Something to do with his father, that terrible childhood. I began to picture Kyle as an iceberg, my Adonis merely the tip, the bulk beneath the surface ready to flip at any moment and swamp us little boats in its wake.

The conflict over promiscuity was settled last year on an October night, the final one we were to have to ourselves before Diane came to San Francisco for good. He and I were having cosmos out on the deck, observing the disaster across the bay—billowy gray towers of smoke, from their insides a red, sinister glow that burst at times into bright-yellow flames. It had burned like that for days. Already people were calling it the Great Oakland Firestorm of 1991.

Nearby, in the Castro, another kind of conflagration: all those beautiful runaways, the men who fled to the city seeking freedom, reduced now to scarecrows.

All the signs now pointed to a new phase, Kyle said, gesturing to the dual spectacles below. The days of profligate

114

sex were over. That word, *profligate*, sounded so old-fash-
ioned, almost biblical. We locked hands and swore an oath
to monogamy, while men died, practically at our feet, and
across the bay houses were reduced to coal and ash.

+ + +

ON THE FOURTH OF JULY, I took it as my patriotic duty
as a citizen of the burgeoning latte nation of San Francisco
to instruct Diane on the operation of my Domobar. Given its
complexity, I didn't see the harm. I never believed she would
get so attached to making espresso. Wouldn't a woman like
that be content with her Sanka?

Pretty soon, though, Kyle and I would be awoken
promptly at 6:30 a.m. by Diane downstairs in our kitchen,
revving up the Rancilio grinder, banging the portafilter on
the butcher block. We didn't need the alarm anymore.

I drew the line at weekends, when I allowed myself to
sleep in, and Kyle, of course, if he didn't have to be on-site.
His new job had become less about being on the boards, as
he called it, and more about construction administration,
something that could be 24–7.

Almost immediately, Diane's coffee making was accompanied by homemade baked goods, which she prepped
downstairs in her apartment the night before. By the middle
of the month, she began each of our weekdays with a full
breakfast. She and Kyle were a couple of June Cleavers

115

reading their papers around our big glass table and I, growing fatter by the day, the lone, hapless Ward.

End of July, Diane fired the maid, a woman who had worked for me the ten years I'd lived in the city. Diane said having a housekeeper was a needless expense. I had to admit my Filipina did an unexceptional job and that our place, after Diane got through with it, had never looked better. The polished stainless steel Domobar, freed from its patina of smudges, gleamed like the beacon of industrial design it was.

Obviously, Diane was making herself indispensable, so even though I wanted to, I couldn't kick her out. I was wise to her master plan. I just didn't know what to do about it.

✦ ✦ ✦

I HURRIED UP the Muni subway station's broad steps, worried over being late for dinner with Kyle. Even the slightest inconvenience he took as a personal affront. That afternoon, our meeting ran long at the mayor's office. The feds released a boatload of money for prevention outreach and our two staffs were banging out the details.

I rounded the corner onto 18th Street to find Kyle slouched against the front of the Chinese restaurant. Ever the contrarian, he sported a green polyester bomber jacket, zipped to the collar—the hoodie inside cowling his head.

"Hello," I said, "this is 1992 calling. You're dressed so, what? '84? '83?"

"It's comfortable and inexpensive. Wasn't that the point?"

"Actually, I think it was to ape heteronormative concepts of traditional masculinity." I gave him a quick, hungry kiss.

"You're late, Mr Smarty Pants."

"I called the job shack, but you'd gone already."

"I wanted to switch out of my dusty clothes, so I left early. The commute's a bitch."

"I wish you could find something in the city."

"It was hard enough finding this job. Well, I didn't find it."

"Technically."

"Rebeca had to call in a lot of chits. I can't ask her to do that again."

Rebeca Vasquez, real estate agent to big East Bay and San Francisco developers. Also Kyle's best friend, also foul-mouthed, improper, doing her best sassy *puertorriqueña*.

"Besides," Kyle said, "business over there is gangbusters with all the rebuilding."

"People died in that fire last year, Kyle. I can't imagine anyone wanting to live there again."

"You've seen the view."

"I know, but to be reminded each day of one's mortality."

"Hard to believe you, of all people, would say something like that."

Over Kyle's shoulder, long fingers of fog snaked around the base of Sutro Tower, the giant robot-looking thing on top of Twin Peaks. Soon the Castro neighborhood would be choked with mist, the houses mysterious hulks, indistinct.

"Come on," he said, "I'm getting cold."

I pushed open the door and we stepped inside the narrow restaurant. A single aisle ran down the center; heavy wooden cubicles were arrayed on either side. The smell of garlic and fish sauce wafted from the kitchen. The synth-pop band Erasure crackled from a pair of blown speakers.

We slid into one of the booths, the high enclosure cave-like, the benches hard and uncomfortable. When the waiter brought the menus, I waved them away and placed the order. "Oh, and two Tsingtao," I said over my shoulder as he walked off. I turned and met Kyle's scowling face. "I'm sorry. Did you want something else? We always get the same thing."

His look, somewhere between a pout and a grin, I read as resignation. Then he laughed and blew me a kiss across the table. The changeability of his moods frequently gave me whiplash.

"I don't mean to emasculate you," I said.

"Rebeca says it's important for May-December relationships to be on an equal footing."

"You and I, we're more May-August, I think. September, at the very latest."

A smile blossomed across his boyishly handsome face. This was the affable guy I preferred, warm-hearted, funny even, when he let down that long brassy-brown hair.

The moo shu pork arrived, along with its little container of pancakes. I slathered hoisin sauce on one and wrapped it loosely around the pork-and-cabbage concoction. Juice dribbled down my fingers as I ate.

The budding architect across from me, after neatly arranging on his pancake a line of the mixture, folded it at one end and rolled it tightly. When he bit into the pancake, there was not a single drip. I wished my employees had this level of meticulousness, though applied to Chinese food it seemed slightly ridiculous.

Cocking his head, Kyle raised his eyebrows and examined me.

"What?" I said.

"I'm trying to decide if I like you with a chin."

I ran my hand down my smooth, recently shaved face. "A strong one, or so they say."

"They?"

"You know, all those other ones." I fluttered my lashes at him coquettishly.

"I don't like to talk about that."

"Oh, come on. I'm just razzing you."

"Well, please don't."

Other couples filtered into the restaurant and slid into booths opposite us. Two women fresh from the office and impeccably dressed in blazers and slacks, a pair of leathermen with chaps over their jeans. Under a raspy Pet Shop Boys song, a dull, rhythmic thud could be heard through the wall from the gay bar next door.

"I hope you haven't forgotten about the cocktail party Thursday night at Bradley's." I tonged another pancake onto his plate with my chopsticks.

He rolled his eyes to the ceiling. "That queen."

"That queen donated nearly a million dollars last year and he absolutely adores you."

"He's so handsy, Robert."

"Just close your eyes and think of England, sweetheart. Every guy there will match what he gives."

"You told me I didn't have to do that stuff anymore. That I was too old to be a trophy wife."

"I was joking."

"About being too old or the trophy wife?"

"Both."

He shook his head and sighed, a veritable stereotype of disgust. "You know Thursday's TV night. *Cheers*, *Seinfeld*. Me and Mom have a standing date."

"Speaking of."

"Don't ask."

I gave him my best deadpan, my unstoppable force to his unmovable object.

"No, we haven't found anything yet," he said.

"Kyle."

"You know how hard it is to rent in our neighborhood."

"Exactly. That's why you need to get on the stick. There's only a month and a half left. Have you even looked?"

"Some."

"I have been patient, Kyle. I have made allowances."

"Allowances?" he said, clearly indignant.

"I let you move in when you were homeless. I wasn't expecting that, or your mother. Or the fucking monogamy, now it comes to it. Sure, I see the logic. My prevention people have been harping about it for years."

"I thought you did those things because you loved me."

"It's just gotten so complicated, Kyle."

"Yeah, like you whoring me out to your donors." The veins of his muscular neck bulged more than they usually did. His lips were lifted slightly in a sneer.

"I am simply asking you to stand around with a bunch of amiable guys and drink free booze and smile. Plus, make some effort to find your mother an apartment. Or I will."

"Is that a threat?"

"Given where we currently stand, I'd say it's more of a promise."

"Oh, let's not argue anymore. It's giving me a headache. Let's go next door and dance. It's our one night off from Mom. We're supposed to be having fun."

"We are." I gestured to the mess between us, the empty platters and bottles of beer. "And look at this place. Just like me, cheap, but fashionable."

"You are neither of those things, Robert. And I mean that as a compliment."

✦ ✦ ✦

THE NEXT MORNING, while Kyle was at Mark's studying for an upcoming licensing exam, Diane was parked in one of the leather chairs across from me at the large glass-topped table where we served all our meals. Looming above her on the back wall was the enormous painting Kyle insisted I buy, a ghostly reclining figure, dry-brushed quickly onto the white canvas so that it looked as if it were made of smoke.

Diane ate from a bowl the dried Mission figs she loved so much and worked on her postcards. A chronic scribbler—sometimes as many as three cards a day—she let them pile up before mailing off a chunk. She always cupped her hand over the cards while she wrote and then squirreled them away, so I never knew who she was corresponding with.

I slurped my latte and stared out the large window at what would sometimes be a spectacular scene. The bay, sugar-frosted on blustery days, marbled when calmed, bisected by the loopy catenaries of the Bay Bridge. Now, though, the fog drew across the frame a damp white sheet, washing out everything in its pale light. Even Diane's hair under its white blaze had turned a muddied bronze.

Diane looked up from her writing with an expression that I would take in another person to be wistful. I noted, speaking to her gingerly over the delicious frittata she had prepared, that if she applied half as much energy as she did caring for our place, and us, by now she could have located five apartments.

Her pen hovering over the postcard she was writing, she told me that helping her son and me make a gracious home gave her a sense of purpose.

It was here that I came up with a counter to her master plan. Even with no apartment in sight, I could still get her out from underfoot, preferably on weekends, when I could have a little unobstructed me time with my lover's hot bod.

I suggested she work at the AIDS helpline run by my organization, saying I knew they needed to fill Saturday and Sunday shifts. She cocked her head and smiled. It seemed she had been waiting for a proposal such as this, and now it had arrived, she accepted it with what could only be described as magnanimity.

She was an instant hit at work. The twinks and leather-men in the call room certified her a total hoot. The drag queens started twanging her folksy expressions in their shtick. They took her shopping at all their top secret thrift stores, where, now her divorce had gone through, Diane spent like crazy on outrageous outfits. Marketing even featured her in next year's calendar shoot—in full leather drag, no less, with an entourage of musclemen. The remnants of the repressed army wife were now totally obliterated.

Though this freed up our weekends somewhat, Diane was soon even more underfoot, volunteering on weekdays as well, so I now had to contend with her both at home and at work. Our intimate breakfasts at the house dried up, with her baking only for the days she pulled shifts in the call room.

I had to pass by there to get to my office. I'd see her seated at one of the long folding tables dolled up like Madonna in a spiky leather dress, doling out her wares, cracking people up in her countrified patter. Or on the phone, listening intently while leafing through her resource book.

+ + +

AS SEPTEMBER APPROACHED, Diane was still living in the downstairs apartment. My repeated inquiries were met with baffled expressions, flurried excuses, piles of inter-vening commitments. In addition to the hotline, she began volunteering at the Buddhist hospice around the corner from our office. There was no time for apartment hunting now that she was Mother Fucking Teresa.

By the end of the week, I'd about had it. In addition to the problems on the home front, we lost two longtime employees to AIDS, men only in their twenties, one who'd been pre-med, the other who'd been pursuing advanced degrees in public health, just as I had.

I kept it together all day, but after work a depression began to blanket me, as chilling as the fog racing above me on Market Street. I plodded up the sidewalk, thinking a quick drink before going home might lift my spirits. Strictly off-limits were any of the *hot* bars, where a row of humpy men at the counter would be getting toasty, their ties dangling from open collars. Being sex-starved with Kyle, I was afraid what might happen.

Instead, I went to what our young volunteers unkindly called a "wrinkle bar," a place for older men to socialize where we won't feel judged. Antiques and comfortable couches lined picture windows that looked out onto the intersection of Castro and Market.

As I was flagging the server at the bar, I heard my name. Rebeca Vasquez pushed her way toward me through the crush of thirsty men. She wore a black, low-cut suit, cinched at her waist by a belt of silver loops. Cradling her angular face, her magenta scarf fairly lit up against her dark skin, the beauty mark on her cheek like a beacon catching my gaze.

"Rebeca, what a nice surprise. What are you doing here?"

"I'm with a client," she said in her lilting Puerto Rican accent. "We've been with his numbers guy all afternoon and he wanted to unwind here. He's someone you need to know, Stollar. He's got more money than God."

I caught the bartender's eye and offered to buy her and her client a round. "Glenlivet, neat," she said. "Maker's Mark. Water backs."

The server, a bespectacled, middle-aged man with the appearance of a librarian, piloted precise amounts of peat-colored liquid into cut glasses.

"I hear Kyle's doing well," Rebeca said.

"Oh?"

"That's the scuttlebutt. I'm putting together some parcels over there for his boss."

"Yeah, he seems to like all the hands-on stuff. How are the girls?" I said, referring to the two women, her lovers, with whom she lived.

"Fine, I guess. One's running Outward Bound workshops in the Sierras all summer. The other's back at Stanford. The Hoover Institute. God, Stollar. I'm married to a Republican! At least I get to see her, even if it's only once in a while."

"Sounds divine. The once-in-a-while part, I mean."

"Trouble at home? How is mommy dearest?"

"Still there, only more so. Now she's volunteering at my organization."

"And whose brilliant idea was that?"

"Mine. I thought it'd get her out of the house on the weekends. Who knew she would make it her life's work?"

"I don't suppose you socialize much anymore, then. Or was it just me who got eighty-sixed by Kyle?"

"It's everybody, really. He comes home tired after a long day at the building site and all he wants to do is hang out with Mom. I know she's the life of the party. Everyone at work adores her, but…"

"But?"

The server lined the glasses in front of us. Short, short, tall. Short, tall. Like the windows in my father's buildings, the rigid patterns I found so dispiriting.

"Let's just say, it's complicated. That's my standard reply."

Rebeca encircled the glasses in her hands. "Oh? We taking that as our new nickname, are we? Robert 'It's Complicated' Stollar?"

"Looks like."

She eyed the drinks intently while stepping back from the bar. "Well, good luck with that. At least come say hi to my client."

I followed her back to a little alcove under a balcony. Ensconced there on a velvet-upholstered couch sat the hedge fund manager from Schwab, my ex-boyfriend. Though not especially handsome, he appeared regal and sporty with his gray goatee, plaid slacks and the yellow cashmere sweater I once loved to strip off him in our whirlwind lead-up to sex.

His face lit up when he saw me approach. "Robert, darling. You look fabulous."

We kissed on the lips a little longer than I'd planned.

"And here I'd prepared this big intro," Rebeca said. "Is there anyone in the city you haven't fucked, Stollar?"

"It's such a small town, really," my friend said, taking the drink she offered him. "We don't count all those wage slaves swarming in every day from the boonies."

I glanced, discreetly I hoped, at my watch. "I just came by to say hello. I've got to get back."

"Call of hearth and home, is it?" my friend said.

"Robert is henpecked," Rebeca said. "Times two. It's a mother-and-son act."

My friend tilted his head, peered down his nose, his eyes scanning the length of my body. "Oh, how I know. It's a great tragedy."

I knocked back my drink, said my goodbyes and headed up the hill toward the house. The streetscape inclining before me dissipated into the fog that swirled and eddied under each streetlamp. In between the pools of light were dim shapes of houses silhouetted against the gray mists.

The more I walked, the more worked up I got over the situation with Kyle's mother, which had devolved, I realized, into stealth warfare. Their intransigence wasn't simple foot-dragging, but a willful contradiction of my wishes. My pace quickened; the closer I huffed to home, the more determined I became to do something about Diane.

Halfway up the hill, my pager beeped. My hedge fund manager: *Ditching dyke. Home in 20. Cum by for quickie.*

His house was only a few blocks from ours. I was tempted. He was easy fun during sex, a conjurer of strange— tantalizing positions, sexy wordplay. Kyle was a bit of a cold fish in the sack, like many of the really good-looking men I've hooked up with. It was the price they paid to head off all the excess devotion they tended to attract.

I punched a *No*, followed by *Thank you.*

Come on, answered the tiny backlit panel. *U know you want it.*

With the options on my cheap pager limited to a handful of canned responses, I toggled off the temptation, then lengthened my stride.

When I mounted the concrete steps to our house, the lights were off in the downstairs apartment, but our place was lit up like Christmas. I heard music, laughing. Inside, it smelled of cilantro and chili. In the kitchen, Diane poured what looked like lemonade into our blender. The *chunk chaka chunk* of electric guitars played on the stereo, under a country singer mooning over some girl that had gone and done him wrong.

"Ahoy there," Diane said. A rhinestone tiara crowned her red-headed majesty, corralling the tuft of white above her forehead.

A tutu of stiff pink tulle splayed out at her waist over black tights that tapered into red high-tops. She looked like an escapee from some weird inversion of elementary school. The only thing that tethered her to the real world was the CAPTAIN STOLLAR T-shirt she wore, and even that was mostly fantastical, a gag beginning to sour.

The blender whirred, the ice crushing in the glass jar making a clicking sound. Kyle bounded down the stairs from the living room. As he did, Diane fired up the blender a second time in quick, short pulses. I jumped.

"Settle down there, partner," Kyle said. "You're just in time for a drink. There's some of Mom's famous enchiladas in the kitchen, if you're hungry." He leaned in and gave me a chaste kiss. "Smells like you already got started, Mister."

"I ran into Rebeca Vasquez at Twin Peaks," I said, as if this would explain my whiskey breath. "You need to call her."

"Yeah, I know." Kyle snapped his head in his mother's direction. "Not right now, though. We're all about to play Scrabble."

The game board was set up on the white glass tabletop, tiles facedown on the grid, wooden racks like opposing armies lined up on three sides.

"*Buenos noches*," Diane said in her perky Texas accent. She was holding a tray with three festively colored cocktail glasses that I'd never seen before. Inside each, under a salted rim, pooled a sickly-green liquid. "Folks, it's margarita time!"

On the stereo, now a woman sang about missing the wide nighttime sky smeared with diamonds, hitting the high notes at an ear-splitting volume.

"Could we please turn that off," I said. "I didn't know you liked country music, Diane."

"We're Texans, Robert, at night to early in the morn. You can't escape it."

"Sure. But not right now." I strode to the stereo and punched the power button.

"Margarita, Kyle." Diane offered her son the tray, her honeyed voice dripping in cornpone.

Kyle took a glass, his eyes darting to me warily.

"Robert, honey?" She held out the tray, shooting me a studied smile. "They're awful good."

From her T-shirt, the imprint of my face stared back at me, misshapen, crushed between her breasts. I had lost my shape too, slowly over the last year, with each day a ratcheting-down of my individuality and agency. I glanced around the room. So familiar, the marble breakfast bar, the line of white leather chairs on either side of the gleaming glass tabletop, Kyle's huge, slightly menacing-looking painting dominating the back wall. I couldn't recognize myself in a single thing.

"I'm going upstairs. Kyle, I need to talk to you."

"Suit yourself," Diane said with an expression that made her seem as if she might actually be hurt.

She placed the tray on the dining table and sat at the Scrabble board, picked several tiles and began to fill her rack. Kyle hovered by the breakfast bar, appearing unsure of what to do.

"You're going to miss out on all the fun." Diane arranged the tiles in her rack, leapfrogging them one by one.

"Stringing words together without meaning isn't my kind of fun," I said.

She lifted her glass by the stem, her pinkie finger shooting straight at me. "And what would your kind of fun be, Robert?"

"Mom," Kyle said, "please. Just leave it."

"No, I'm interested. Because I don't see a lot of fun around here lately."

All this was delivered along with the most benevolent of smiles. I found the Texas charm bone-chilling.

I glanced at Kyle. The pleading on his face was deeply unattractive. "Kyle, can I have a word?"

Diane drew her last tile from the board. "Such a drama queen."

"Excuse me?" I said.

"I'm sorry. Did I not use that expression correctly?" Diane turned to her son and gave him a wink.

I pounded up the stairs into the living room, Kyle in pursuit. "Honey," he said. "She's just messing with you."

I spun around to face him. "You haven't done a fucking thing to get her out of here, have you?"

Kyle lowered his head and clasped his hands in front of his crotch, a childish gesture, so incongruous on his big, manly body. "No. Not really."

"Did you think I was going to forget?"

"You don't understand. Everything we've gone through."

"Because you haven't fucking told me. Whatever happened back in Texas, wouldn't that be something you'd want to share with your partner?"

"I'm trying to forget all that."

"You can't have it both ways, Kyle."

His face flushed, the veins protruded on the sides of his neck again, alerting me to the imminent blastoff. I grabbed him by the shoulder when he turned to leave.

"You think I won't understand? I know all there is about unhappy childhoods, Kyle. About demanding, disappointing fathers."

He placed a hand on my chest and knit his brows together. "No, darlin'. You don't know a goddam thing about it."

I sighed, let my head fall back onto my shoulders. I gazed at the ceiling's white plane, straining to see in that blankness what Kyle found so comforting. I had the impression instead that I was in one of those dreams I used to have as a child, wandering some interminably long hall of an ancient house. Then falling abruptly, afraid, no bottom in sight, to awake crying in a room I no longer recognized.

I jolted back into the present. On Kyle's face now, that same awful blankness, the vacant-eyed, slack look. He was receding into his icy fortress. I enveloped him in my arms, all I could think to do to keep him from disappearing entirely. I was in the business of saving people. Why did I find it so difficult to save Kyle?

I could feel his shoulders lower and his body relax. When I pulled away from him, the liveliness had returned to his face.

"Bear with me, please," he said. "With us. With the new job and Mom coming, it's been overwhelming. I'll take a couple of days off. I promise, we'll look for apartments."

I gave him a perfunctory kiss, much too tired for anything else. "I'm going upstairs to take a pill and knock myself out. You coming?"

"In a minute. Let me play awhile with Mom. She's been looking forward to this all day." His smile seemed cunning, a display of agreeableness that came off Stepford Wives creepy.

On the top floor, I flung myself into bed without bothering to turn on the lights. An eerie white glow illuminated the bedroom, the streetlamp opposite the window shrouded in fog. I could hear Diane and Kyle talking downstairs, the country tune on the stereo taking up where it had let off.

It used to be so quiet up here at night in my little treetop retreat, my empty house below pressed against the slope of Twin Peaks. Back when I was single, I hated it. When Kyle had called from the pay phone on Castro five years earlier to confess that he was living in his car, I could hear the desperation in his voice and was glad.

I craved a return to that quiet's predictability, to reclaim myself as best I could. I didn't put much stock in my lover's promise. Over the weekend, I'd book Diane into a bed and breakfast or, if I couldn't find one on such short notice, a hotel. A nice one. I wasn't vindictive. From there, we'd see how things went.

Now, I needed a little space. The bracing night air—dank and cold though it might be. Some easy fun. A taste of strange.

I rose, padded to the closet and slipped into my sweats. I laced up my running shoes. I switched my pager back on and clipped it to the waistband of my pants. On this high side of the long house, there was another exit, a flight of wooden stairs that I could use to slink unnoticed out onto the street above.

Diane

SEATED AT HER writing desk, Diane signs a loopy *D* at the bottom of the postcard she has just scrawled to her daughter. The upset the previous evening with her son moved Diane to write—rather perversely, she feels, given that she blames Rachel for Kyle's delicate mental state. She blames the season as well. The beginning of May is always bad for him.

Outside her window, the fog, so unusual in San Francisco at this time of year, has retreated and the weather is fine. From her vantage point atop Potrero Hill, through a screen of tree limbs, she watches the beige towers of downtown glint in the afternoon sun. These comfort her, Kyle and his new partner, Jason, working away down there now to support their beautiful life. She in her new apartment in the coach house out back, they in the remodeled Victorian up front, on Texas Street, of all places.

She flips over the postcard: on the cover a vineyard out-side Calistoga where she and the boys took a recent trip. She is unsure why she continues to write her daughter. Over the last five months there has been only a trickle of replies. If you could even call them that. Typed single-spaced on a photocopy of a postcard Diane had previously sent, each described a little scene featuring Rachel, Diane and Kyle set in the picture on the cover.

In the one from Sebastopol, in an oceanside park along a high cliff, Kyle balances on top of a picnic table, reciting lines from the Shakespeare play they've just attended. He does a hilarious, over-the-top Ophelia, even crying real tears!

In another letter, paired with a photo of Half Moon Bay, a charming but down-on-his-luck private detective books a case with a femme fatale—an obvious version of Rachel, only tall, heavily endowed, with an hourglass figure. The woman's brother and his male lover were found at a sleazy beachside motel—in bed naked, arms and legs inter-twined—with two shots each in the head. Unsurprisingly, their mother did it. Something about her belonging to a religious sect.

Five years earlier, when Diane moved to the city, she kept these cards she wrote her daughter free of particulars, especially her address. Diane was fearful of Rachel spilling the beans to her father. Fearful he'd then dispatch some army goons to retrieve his errant wife, his interest in her finally piqued by her abandonment. She'd rather throw herself on a grenade than be dragged back to that godforsaken place. Fort Hood. Killeen. Texas.

After she reclaimed her maiden surname during her divorce, synchronizing it with her son's; after Kyle's ex, that snake Robert, kicked her out of her apartment, she thought— why not? Within a week of firing off to Rachel a card with a return address, there came a box of the strange replies.

On the back of the postcard she's just written her daughter, Diane adds a postscript. The same one she attaches to each note: *It's just not a good time for a visit, Rachel. Your brother is working hard to clean up his act.*

Why did she write this last part? Kyle is doing great. A new job, a new partner. Robert finally ditched: he of the roving eye, the wayward member. On top of her general distaste for the man, when Robert was with her son, she feared for Kyle's safety. She's seen up close at the hospice where promiscuity can lead. Her son deserves better and, though Jason is far from perfect, now he has it.

She adds Rachel's card to the stack to be mailed the following day—Saturday, her day for shopping—then shuffles through some blank ones, searching for a card to send to her mother. Diane decides on one of her poor de Young Museum, since the Loma Prieta shaker practically falling apart, like her mother. Apparently. Other than their family's tendency to avoid unpleasantness, Diane can imagine no other reason why Elaine should be so evasive in her replies, seemingly papering over some unmentionable calamity.

141

After composing an equally vague response to her mother, Diane thumbs the adhesived stamps onto the cards. She pushes the chair back from her writing desk. Crossing the living room, she inhales the smell of new: new paint, new furniture and appliances. The divorce money. And curiously—though her father isn't exactly a skinflint— the old man had been lavishly generous.

Diane descends the stairs to the ground floor, carefully. Though only fifty-five, her hips have begun to trouble her. She locks her front door and winds across the flagstones in the lower garden. It is a little trampled down from all the remodeling, but has good bones. Several types of hostas and ferns are shaded by a large, rather prehistoric-looking Norfolk Island pine. In its branches, a crow croaks a greeting.

Diane has long since given up housework. She insists, though, on reclaiming this little area herself, since gardening was never possible living on base at Fort Hood. With having to care for the boys, though, she hasn't yet gotten around to it.

She plods up the bouncy wooden stairs to the top deck and props herself for a moment against the rail, which always feels to her like flying. Up here on Potrero Hill, she hovers above the converted warehouses of the design district. Past that, the highway frames the eastern limit of SoMa and the office towers beyond.

How beautiful this view, these houses in which she, her son and his new partner live. How far from dusty Venable

Village she has come. Now, her acquaintances aren't army wives with a bunch of snotty brats in tow, but retired teachers from the AIDS helpline and hospice, fellow docents at the beleaguered but still open de Young. The friends who come to the house for the dinners she prepares are no longer noncommissioned ignoramuses, but the boys' colleagues—designers, architects. And Kyle's brash, hilarious Puerto Rican friend, Rebeca, with the two lovers who often accompany her.

Now, when Diane goes bowling, as she was so often required to do in Killeen, the alley is black-lit and Day-Gloed, thumping with a head-spinning techno. And though the years living in the city have worn away the giddiness she felt on her arrival, she still sports her thrift store finds—only classics now, gray Chanel suits, or, as she does today, a black ankle-length YSL ruffled dress. A little much for dining *en famille*, as Kyle now likes to say, but, to make up for last night's unpleasantness, she has decided to treat their evening ritual as a special occasion.

She lets herself into the boys' house with her key. In the kitchen, she slips the rack of lamb from the fridge and stows it on the butcher block counter under the antique brass factory lamps. Jason and Kyle have gone for an industrial aesthetic. Open black wire racks instead of kitchen cabinets. For dining, a large, heavily used fabric-cutting table, hemmed in by galvanized metal stools. Monopolizing the long sidewall is one of the few things Kyle insisted on retaining from Robert's—the painting of the sinister-looking figure hovering on its side.

She douses oil on the Brussels sprouts and new potatoes she previously halved, then arranges them, along with the lamb, on a baking sheet lined with parchment paper. At 6:20, she slides the pan in the preheated oven. She retrieves the bottle of gin from the freezer, along with the frosted metal martini glasses. Filling each with the viscous liquid, adding a splash of vermouth, a skewer of olives, she hears the key click in the front door.

Diane greets her son in the entry hall with his cocktail. He removes his sports coat and tosses it on the newel post at the foot of the stairs, a habit of his that annoys her. His new short hair, though, meets with her approval. More in keeping, she thinks, with a man of his station.

He loosens his tie then unbuttons the collar of his shirt. He takes the martini she proffers by the glass's frosted metal stem. "Just what I need, Mom. Jason back yet?"

"He called to let me know he'll be a little late. Such a polite boy."

"Mostly."

"Now, now." She clanks the rim of her metal glass against his. "If you can't say anything nice..."

Drinks in hand, they stroll out onto the deck. Though it is generally warm under clear skies at the beginning of May, fog has stormed the bastion of Twin Peaks and is marauding below them now through the Castro and the Mission.

"How was work?" she says. Her voice retains its staccato cadence, though its overall flavor is no longer quite so obviously Texan.

"Oh, you know." Kyle lies back on one of the padded lounge chairs and nestles his head on the palm of one hand.

"You're sick of me saying this," she says, "but I am just so proud of you. An architect. A designer at a big firm."

"It's a midsized firm, Mother. You know that. And Jason's the designer. I'm just a job captain."

"Job Captain Turner! Well, doesn't that sound grand. I know it's from a different service branch, but how ironic... It makes you sound like your father, Sergeant Major Asshole."

"And we've been doing so well lately."

"Sorry to bring him up. It just slipped out. I mean, it happened. We can't ignore it."

"We can try."

Whatever her feelings for her ex-husband, Diane finds it difficult to refrain from speaking about him. Now that Kyle is in his mid-thirties, his hair is brown like his father's, his face similarly broadened with age, the same square jaw, the bedroom eyes. There is a certain brittleness, too, in both their personalities from struggling so long to keep their darker aspects at bay. On occasion, Kyle looks and acts so like his father she has to turn aside.

Through the open doorway, they hear Jason clump into the living room, toss his briefcase onto the cutting table.

145

"Hello, the house!" Jason bounds onto the deck, holding the waiting martini he has retrieved from the freezer. He pecks Kyle on the lips and Diane on each cheek, then collapses onto the lounge chair between them.

He is an excitable twenty-six. His ancestry is suggested by—Diane isn't sure exactly. A narrowing and upturn of his eyes, perhaps, but so slight it is easy for her not to notice. The same is true of his charming but somewhat rigid Japanese-American mother, who Diane met once, along with her husband, a pallid, opinionated stick of a man.

Jason did not inherit his mother's beauty. He has a slightly asymmetrical face, obscured by thick-rimmed glasses that hang on his broad nose under heavy brows. He is dressed in the fashion of the moment for young men: below-the-knee khaki shorts, Tevas with ankle-length socks. To ward off the early summer chill, he wears a faded, fleece-lined denim vest over a tight white T.

"That outfit's a bit extreme, even for dress-down Fridays," Kyle says.

"I had early meetings, so I took off at three and hit the gym."

"You trying to make me feel guilty?" Kyle pats the growing cushion at his belly.

"Not at all. You've done your duty, sir." Jason reaches over and clutches one of Kyle's large biceps. "Diane, sorry we have to dash to the opera tonight. We're very excited. Aren't we, Kyle?"

Kyle sips his martini, while pondering the view of downtown that is beginning to be curtained by wisps of fog.

"Oh yes, Cecilia Bartoli," Diane says. "I understand she's a very big deal."

"She better be," Jason says. "Good thing Sweetcheeks here got that new job, so he can pitch in with the tickets."

Kyle frowns into his flared metal glass. "Sweetcheeks?"

"Oh, I don't know...I'm just auditioning it. My mother says it to my dad sometimes. Pretty sure she does it to piss him off."

"Yeah," Kyle says, "well, I know exactly how he feels."

Jason prods his last olive from the toothpick and pops it in his mouth. "You aren't going to get like last night, are you?"

"And how's that?"

"Oh, you know. In one of your moods. Grouchy."

Kyle leaps to his feet. "It's been a hard day. I'm going to lie down before supper."

"Darling," Diane says, checking her wristwatch. "It'll just be a little bit."

"Can I have friggin' ten minutes to myself, please?" Kyle pounds into the house and vanishes up the stairs.

"Jason, dear," Diane says.

"Yes, Mother." Jason bows his head to his chest in a display of mock contrition.

"Don't *Yes, Mother* me, young man," Diane says, laying back on the Texas twang. Though faded, she still dials it up on occasions like this: to entertain, to chastise.

"I was only joking."

"Apparently, he didn't get the memo."

"He's so blinkin' sensitive."

"This should not be news to you by now."

Ten minutes pass. No Kyle. Returning to the kitchen, Diane pulls the baking sheet from the oven. Everything done to perfection.

"I better see what's going on," Jason says, abandoning his empty glass on the butcher block.

Diane does a quick table setting, using the fluted glass-ware, the good china and cutlery, while the phantom in the painting on the wall looms over her. Fifteen minutes later, she eases the food back in the oven to warm then heads upstairs to investigate. Through the open doorway, she finds Jason dressed in a gray suit sitting on the edge of the bed next to Kyle. Her son's eyes are closed. He's lying on his side, faced away from Jason.

"Honey," Jason says, "they won't seat us until intermission if we're late. Let's grab a quick bite and go. Cecilia Bartoli, babe. You love her Despina."

When Kyle buries his head in the stack of pillows, Jason's face flushes. "Come on, now. We've waited six months for this, not to mention the seven hundred dollars."

Nothing.

Jason is yelling at her son now. "I fucking can't stand this. I kept thinking it was the pressure from the new job, from the house remodel, but this..."

Kyle opens his eyes. He looks, not at Jason, but at Jason's portrait hanging by the side of the bed in its simple black frame. Kyle retired his sketchbooks for good right after he finished it—three years ago, when he and Jason first met. In the portrait, the excitement on Jason's face can be plainly seen, in contrast to his present pinched and angry look.

Jason jumps to his feet, spins around and faces Diane, who is positioned near the door. She fixes him with her best imperious stare. Reaching out, with a flick of a finger, she brands his forehead with a long painted nail.

The sound of it striking Jason's skull is unexpectedly loud. He winces, pushes past her into the hall.

She pulls the door closed behind him. "He's fine. Just overworked is all. And you know how he gets this time of year." The angularity of her exaggerated Texas drawl is as pointed as daggers. She waves Jason down the corridor with a fluttering hand. "Don't even ask. All that caterwauling gives me headaches."

Heavy footsteps on the stairs. The front door slams.

She prepares her son a tray and he eats in bed, she seated in a chair nearby, picking at a bowl of roasted vegetables. She reads her whodunit while Kyle meditates, or whatever he does in these states, eyes shut or else staring at the ceiling. After some time, she doesn't know how long, she tiptoes across the squeaky floorboards to the guest bathroom and pees. The entry door below creaks open. On the stairway, Jason's footfalls softly retrace the worn wooden treads.

Before going downstairs, she hesitates at the top landing. Through the bedroom doorway she catches sight of Jason, in bed leaning against the backboard with Kyle's head in his lap, combing his fingers through her son's short brown hair.

IN THE BEDROOM of her apartment, Diane sits in her slip at the makeup table, reaches behind her to unclasp the single strand of pearls that hangs at her neck. In the mirror, a woman who is beginning to look like her mother. Unlike Elaine, the brassy hair laced with gray, the tuft of white crowning the forehead, Diane refuses to color. But the aging face she obscures under pancake and blush, enlivening the eyes with paint and mascara. She scoops two fingers into the jar then works cold cream onto that face. With tissues, she wipes it away. Unadorned, what remains retains a suggestion of her girlish self—a dusting of freckles on each cheek.

Her thoughts cast back to her twenties—the army base in Korea where she and her husband were stationed right after they married. Military life had been stultifying. Her father warned her, having served in Korea himself during the war. As a consolation, she adored how exotic it was, the times her husband had leave and they took the bus into Daegu—the temples with their upswept tile roofs, the colorful paper lanterns, the cherry blossom springs. That and the fact he was so handsome, such a charmer, always making her laugh.

Images of the afternoon Kyle was conceived came into view. Then, the life of the body finally claimed her and it coupled with a love she had never known. The love a woman has for her husband. Shyly lustful, protective, proud. After, she lay in bed listening to their rapid breathing, to girls playing hopscotch outside their bedroom window, their singsong verse, their markers clattering on the concrete sidewalk. She shivered when, with the back of a finger, her husband lightly traced the line of her jaw. How seductive that time. How devastating its loss.

IN THE MORNING, she wakes feeling listless. She does a few stretches in the living room, then prepares coffee in the French press. While the boys sleep in, she backs down the drive the Beamer that the three of them share and heads to what people call the Gay Safeway. The one on Market Street. In the median, recently planted Canary palms bristle their green, feathery wings from scaly trunks and spread them over four lanes of traffic. From her view in the parking lot, the palms appear to be parading headless angels. Guardian angels, she thinks. Unlike her husband, only in her childhood has she been even the slightest bit devout. Still, this notion pleases her.

And as if the angels are manifesting her latent desires, inside the supermarket—hypnotized by can after can of processed meats and vegetables—Diane wheels her half-empty cart around the end of the aisle and runs into her daughter. She almost knocks Rachel over.

Diane hovers for a moment between recognition and disbelief. She hasn't seen her daughter in five years. Rachel appears stricken, but is smiling in a way that seems oddly rehearsed.

Diane opens her mouth and is embarrassed when nothing comes out. "What the hell are you doing here?" she says finally. She is aware that this sounds unkind.

Rachel's eyes flutter in their sockets. She shifts her weight from foot to foot. "Actually, I'm living here now."

Diane grips her cart's handlebar more firmly. "You're living here? In San Francisco?"

"Yeah, maybe. I'm sort of trying it out. And not here here exactly. I'm staying in the Outer Mission. I mean really out. Practically Daly City. I can't afford to rent in San Fran."

"We don't say San Fran."

"Oh, sorry."

Diane's knees buckle slightly. She braces herself against a shelf loaded with rows of canned Vienna sausages.

"Mother, are you okay?"

"No, I'm not okay. You springing yourself on me like this."

"It wasn't exactly planned. I've been trying to work up the courage to call."

"Call? How? I never gave you my number."

"Your cell's listed in your AOL profile."

Something Diane doesn't understand how to use or even have a need for, the internet. Jason set it up after they gave her the new flip phone.

"How long?"

"How long what?"

"Have you been living here?"

"Five months."

"Jesus, right under our noses."

"I'm not stalking you, if that's what you think. I'm just off to Stinson Beach for the day and this place is on the way." Rachel addresses the canned corn behind Diane, not having once looked her in the eyes.

Two women approach, pushing a cart brimming with bundled greens in clear plastic bags. Diane rolls her cart to the side. In contrast, hers contains only cheeses and crackers, fruit and sausages, and twenty or so packages of dried Mission figs.

"You still eat those things?" Rachel says.

"Oh yes. Some habits never go away."

"And others?"

"Well, we don't know yet, do we?"

Again, Diane is aware her remark sounds hurtful, but are her daughter's feelings really important? Isn't she the Judas in their family's passion play? It wasn't just the incident with the magazine. Rachel squawked about it to all her little friends at school as well. Then they passed the news to everybody they knew. Soon, all Killeen was calling her son a homo. When they finally kicked Kyle out of that place in Waco, he looked just like her husband had returning from the POW camp. Skinny, vacant-eyed. They had both been hollowed out, only Kyle's torment had just begun. Her son was harassed daily, bloodied and bruised by random strangers. At school, he ate in the lunchroom alone. Even the Boy Scouts wouldn't have him. And now here's Rachel, passing herself off as a supplicant, practically wearing sackcloth—that formless, food-stained sweat suit—no makeup, the badly hacked DIY haircut.

"Look, I can't get into all this now," Diane says. "I have to be back at the house. We're meeting people for a picnic at the Presidio at two."

"How's Kyle?" Rachel blurts this out.

"Really superlative. He's an architect now."

"Wow, that's wild. He never even bothered to open the Erector set Dad gave him."

A frown flits across Diane's face. She reaches into her fanny pack, retrieves the plastic case and pulls from it a business card. "I don't suppose you really need this, but here. Cell's written on the back."

Rachel thumbs the edge of the card. "Helpline Coordinator."

"Long story."

Rachel riffles through her clutch purse and offers Diane her card.

Diane taps it into her holder. "Alaska Airlines? Customer service."

"It's temporary." Rachel closes her eyes and lets out a sigh, as if preparing herself for the magnitude of a coming revelation. When she opens them, she gazes for the first time into Diane's eyes. "For a long while I've been wondering...does Kyle draw anymore?"

IT'S ONLY ELEVEN THIRTY, but after coming across Rachel, Diane needs a cocktail. Not at home. The boys will be off to the gym by now. She doesn't want to drink alone.

Diane abandons the shopping cart in the middle of the aisle, ditches the car in the lot and storms up Market Street. Ahead, the last of the ropy coils of fog is receding over the top of Twin Peaks. Too soon, she thinks, this fog.

When she gets to Castro Street, she finds the sidewalks jammed with people. From all the running around down here you'd hardly think AIDS is still a problem. But it's 1997 and now, with what they call *the cocktail*, boys aren't dying as often as before. She still has her work cut out for her at the helpline, the hospice. The populations are shifting, though—intravenous drug users, closeted bisexual men and their female partners.

Outside the bar at the corner of Market and Castro, she plucks her flip phone from her purse. When she reaches Kyle, he and Jason are already on the bus. She calls a confab. No, she can't discuss it on the phone. Call Bethie and Boffo, or whoever they were meeting for lunch, and cancel. Mandatory attendance. Now.

She ambles through the open door into the bar. On her first visit to the city—the summer a year after Kyle made his getaway, while her son was busing tables—she often came here. She never expected something so cozy in the Castro, a place known for its packed restaurants and murky cruise bars. But the bank of windows let in a barrage of light onto the upholstered couches, antiques, a big mirrored bar.

For a change then, she found herself surrounded by people her own age—nice men, nice clothes and haircuts, a little lonely perhaps, behind all their boisterousness. They smiled at her and winked. Bought her drinks and asked if she needed help. They thought she was a tourist who had wandered in mistakenly. Which, on that first trip, she basically was.

To escape Killeen, on that and every visit after to the city, she spun a tale she'd worked out with her friend Myrtle. The two of them had traveled to Galveston—one of their semi-regular girls' trips to hit the beach and the spa. Though in the end her husband had been too uninterested to question the ruse, on that first trip she was terrified he wouldn't buy it.

She feared also in what condition she might find her son. But Kyle greeted her at the door of his apartment freshly showered and shaved, looking happy in the new clothes she had sent. He showed her the Walkman he'd bought with money his grandfather wired him—so excited about

156

everything Kyle practically leapt out of his skin. He was still only a boy. Her boy, who needed looking after then more than ever.

To keep tabs on him, Diane traveled to the city on three more occasions, before the hiatus her son's early days with Robert inspired. On each of those visits—when Kyle was at school or working at the restaurant or, later, interning at Mark's architecture firm—she wound her way down here to this bar. She'd enter, a hand would fly up, someone would bumble over on his couch and pat the spot next to him. Darling, he'd say. He and his friends would kiss her on the cheek and they'd joke around, happy to be settled in their comfy seats by the windows, while the river of people flowed by outside.

Today, at this early hour, the room is only half-occupied and she notices nobody that she knows. She orders a Tom Collins and proceeds to her favorite couch under the balcony, its red velvet and gold leaf brightly lit in the noonday sun. She frets for a moment about running into Robert. It's bad enough having to face him during her shifts at the helpline. This morning, though, he's probably still in bed, having run amok down here at the bars Friday night.

After a few moments, the boys troop in, each with a petite gym bag dangling from one hand. They grab Bloody Marys at the bar and join her on the couch.

"Jesus, Mom," Jason says. "What's the emergency?"

"Red alert, boys! The demon spawn has blown into town."

"The what?" Kyle says.

"I just ran into your sister at the supermarket."

"What the fuck?" Kyle says.

"Exactly," Diane says. "She appears to have gotten tired of waiting for our invite."

Jason slurps the red liquid noisily through a straw. "Well, that's great news, isn't it? I'm excited to meet her finally."

"Have you forgotten the mess she caused?" Diane says. "You weren't there. You take it so lightly."

"No, I don't. It's just…it was so long ago," Jason says. "You can't still hold that against her, can you, Mom?"

Diane swirls the last of her drink, downs it quickly and plunks the glass on the marble table in front of them. "You know, dear, sometimes when you call me that, it feels like you're—what's the expression?—like you're playing me." Immediately, she is sorry for having said this, for how these hurtful things come so easily from her mouth.

Frowning, Jason stabs the ice in his glass with his celery stick.

"I haven't spoken to Rachel in fifteen years," Kyle says. "What would I say to her? Oh, thank you very much for fucking up my entire life!"

Jason, the poor boy, looks as though he might break in half. "Hey now," he says, "we have a very good life, Kyle."

Kyle takes Jason's hand and kisses it. "I know. See? Already Rachel's messing things up."

"She has a talent for that," Diane says.

"Well, you can't just ignore her," Jason says. "We should invite her to the house. I'll make dinner. I'll channel my grandmother and whip up some killer Japanese."

"Coffee only, on the first date," Diane says. "That's some kind of rule, apparently."

"Is it?" Kyle finishes his drink and slides the tall glass onto the table.

"Robert told me that," Diane says.

"Robert would know," Kyle says.

"Come on," Jason says. "This is a good thing, Rachel coming here. It's a chance. Heal the rift and everything."

"Is that even possible?" Kyle says.

"Of course." Jason raises his glass. "People, let's heal the motherfucking rift."

✦ ✦ ✦

A WEEK OF INDECISION passes, the three of them dreading Rachel's call and not daring to reach out on their own. At the bar, Jason made his thinking clear. Conversation. Connection. Reconciliation.

For Diane, her son is impossible to read. Surely he must want to quit this burden. Over the years his questioning her about his sister has led her to believe so. But the expression of his desires in this, as in all other matters, is never direct.

As for herself, she is prevented from forming an opinion by the ambivalence that has always marred her relationship with her daughter. Back in Killeen, Diane had been determined not to let that interfere with her motherly duties. She chauffeured Rachel to the hundreds of activities of a popular teenager: cheerleading practice, football games, Girl Scouts, sleepovers with friends.

When Rachel left for university in Austin, a distance grew between them that was more than merely geographical. For Diane smarted at the realization that her daughter's ever-decreasing visits were mainly to spend time with her dad, a bland person for whom Diane no longer had any interest. So be it, Diane had thought. She was planning on upending that old life anyway.

Even after she decamped from Texas, telling only her mother of her whereabouts, Diane never severed the connection with her daughter. Those postcards she so dutifully scribbled were lifelines meant to keep them both from slipping under the surface. But she kept Rachel on a long tether. Barely in view and struggling against the current. Diane asks herself, is she capable now of anything more?

Jason finally breaches the impasse and phones Rachel. Their hesitation is making everything bigger than it needs to be, he says. Diane finds this comment naive, but also probably spot-on.

The afternoon Rachel is to visit at their house on Potrero Hill, another letter from her mother arrives. In it, as usual, Elaine limits herself to trivialities—her recent cruises with the women in her book group, the country club goings-on—

but she describes them halfheartedly, almost as if they are hearsay. This lack of conviction hints at some distress, so out of character for the sassy, confident Elaine.

Reclining in the leather lounge chair in the living room, Diane tosses the letter onto a spindly metal side table. She peers out a small window down the slot their house makes with the neighbors'. Over the Mission District below, the early fog billows.

A chill seeps through the gap under the bottom sash and Diane slides closed the window, its counterweights rumbling in their compartments. She draws a comforter she knitted to her chest.

The doorbell rings. Across from her, seated on the couch, Kyle flips another page in the large Richard Avedon coffee-table book. When the bell chimes again, Jason rushes to respond. Ushering Rachel into the entry hall, he positions the two of them at the foot of the stairs.

Diane watches the pair through the arched opening in the living room wall, as if they are performers in a play.

"Hi. So great to finally meet you. I'm Jason," he says, extending one hand.

Rachel is prevented from shaking it by the long-stemmed calla lilies sheathed in clear plastic cradled in her arms. "Jason?"

"We spoke on the phone. Your brother's partner. Husband, really." Jason elevates his left hand to show the ring. "It's not a thing yet, but people are doing it anyway."

"Oh, yeah," Rachel says. "Jason, sure. Sorry. I'm just a little..."

Rachel's eyes dart to the opening to light on Diane. Something like happiness mixed with dread animates her daughter's face. Her shortness of stature is accentuated by how stooped she has become. She wears a striped long-sleeved sweater whose arms protrude from a nondescript-looking jumper. Chubby, stockinged legs terminate in a pair of Birkenstock clogs.

Rachel returns her attention to Jason. She presents him the lilies, hesitates, glances at Diane and pulls back, then again offers Jason the bouquet. He snatches it a little too quickly, Diane thinks. Probably to head off another bout of Rachel's indecision.

"Mother," Rachel says, stationing herself below the arched opening as if she fears entering her son's beautifully appointed house. "You used to love these."

"I recall finding the smell overpowering."

Taking Rachel by the arm, Jason leads her into the living room. "I think you mean Easter lilies, Diane." Jason pokes his nose into one of the trumpet-shaped flowers, so pearly white as to be nearly translucent. He makes a show of breathing in. "See? Nothing." He turns to Rachel and places his hand on her forearm again. "It's a lovely gesture."

When Jason returns from the kitchen with the flowers arranged in a blue ceramic vase, Diane is staring at the wispy fog trailing by the window. Hunched over, Kyle continues to leaf through the Avedon photos. Rachel, who has planted herself in front of the shelves, is running her finger down the spines of a row of books.

Jason places the vase on the dining table and frowns at their little trio. Be careful what you wish for, young man, Diane thinks. You wanted to play peacemaker.

"Kyle," Jason says, "why don't you show your sister around?"

Kyle straightens then stands. He is wearing madras shorts and a tight white knitted shirt.

Witnessing for the first time the length of her brother, Rachel gapes at Kyle, eyes wide. "Wow, look at you! You're a monster. Not a monster... sorry. I don't mean that. You're just really *big*. You used to be such a skinny kid."

The corners of Kyle's mouth bend upward in an expression that does double duty as a smile and a smirk. He trudges into the dining room and takes an upright stance in front of the large painting. Rachel follows him, brows knit, her eyes pleading. Diane finds it pitiful to watch. Kyle launches into a lecture on the importance of the painting's creator. Judging by her confused expression, Rachel looks as put off by the painting's ghostly figure as Diane is.

Kyle leads his sister back into the living room, while haranguing her on the furniture's various designers. Rachel's head pivots as she scans the room.

"Where are your drawings?" she says.

Kyle collapses back onto the couch. "I don't have time for that anymore."

"He sketches these beautiful illustrations of the designs at his firm," Jason says. "Can I get you something to drink, Rachel? Anybody?"

No one.

Jason takes a seat on the couch next to Kyle. "They're just progress drawings, but they really give the designers the feel of the place. It's almost like being there."

"I remember how the shading made the drawings seem alive," Rachel says.

"Oh yes," Jason says, "shading and light are Kyle's specialties. Those computer modelers firms are using now make everything look so sterile." Jason pats the seat of the spartan metal chair next to him and Rachel sits.

Jason's overeagerness is making Diane antsy. She clambers off the lounge chair. "I'm getting a beer. Kyle?"

Kyle nods and resumes paging through the book.

"Rachel, would you like a beer?" Jason says.

"No, I have to be at work in a bit."

"Rachel's in customer service," Diane says over her shoulder as she walks to the kitchen.

Kyle slaps the cover of the book closed and leans back against the couch. "I thought you were in accounting now."

"I'm still looking. It's super competitive here."

From the kitchen, Diane intrudes with a barrage of small talk on the subject of the fabulousness of their life in San

Francisco. A life that doesn't include Rachel, she so unsubtly implies. Where is the softness of her youth, Diane wonders as she cubes a block of cheese. Gone, slipped under the surface. In this too, she is becoming like her mother. She returns to the living room with the necks of three bottles wedged between the fingers of one hand and a cheese plate balanced in the other.

"Accounting must be so fascinating," Jason says.

This might come across as patronizing, Diane thinks, if Jason didn't appear so puppyish and sincere.

"It's not something you can love, really," Rachel says. "It just comes to me easily. The numbers go click, click, click in my head and the answers pop up."

What an odd remark. It's as if her daughter is speaking English but the words won't mount up in a way that others can fully comprehend.

"I'm hopeless at math," Jason says. "You should see me trying to add up dimension strings. One-eighth, five-sixteenths, three thirty-seconds. I can never find the common denominator. I had to take my structures test three times."

"Structures test?" Rachel says.

"One of the architecture licensing exams. Your brother aced his on the first try. I guess the math gene runs in your family."

"Kyle? You were always terrible at math."

"Yeah, well, apparently I test well. I studied, of course. I had help." Kyle slams a draft of his beer then bangs the bottle

165

down on the glass tabletop. "Look, can we all just stop playing nice? Rachel, what the fuck do you want?"

"Come on now," Jason says. "Be polite."

"Why should I? You're doing a hell of a job for all of us."

Rachel rises to her feet, but Jason clasps her by the forearm and urges her back down.

Diane resumes her position on the lounger, draws a fingertip down the contours of her pearl necklace. "Why did you give up mathematics, anyway? Your teachers thought you were some kind of Einstein."

"I liked it better early on, I guess. Geometry, algebra, trig. Back when it was more like solving puzzles, not trying to fathom all the mysteries of the blinkin' universe. I mean, it wasn't a total loss. The accounting career. Plus, now I'm a total Sudoku whiz."

Jason pinches a cube of cheese from the plate, tosses it into his mouth and laughs. "Your sister's a hoot, Kyle. You never told me she was so funny."

"I never told you anything about her, except that she destroyed my fucking life."

"Stick to the plan, honey. Heal the rift, remember? Let's not get melodramatic."

"And how should we get, Jason?"

"Kyle, stop acting like a child. I'm not the bad guy here."

"Look, this isn't working," Rachel says. "It's a lot, I know. Me just showing up out of nowhere. I'd hoped... Well, I need to catch the four-thirty bus anyway. I'm pulling the evening shift from home."

"Have a nice life," Kyle says. He storms into the kitchen, snatches another beer from the fridge then darts out on the back deck.

"Kyle," Jason calls after him. "Honey."

Diane observes her daughter rising slowly to her feet. Rachel's head has drifted downward slightly, her shoulders slumped under the gray jumper. Always considering her the villain has sheltered Diane from her own responsibility in their family's story and from Rachel's feelings, but she hadn't cared. She isn't sure she cares even now. Seeing how guarded her daughter has become, though, how timid, when once she was such a hellion, a feeling washes over Diane that spawns a welter of words she struggles to comprehend.

Jason scrambles off the couch. "I better go see about Kyle." He leans over and plants a kiss on Rachel's cheek. "This was so brave. I promise, it will get easier."

"You think so?" Rachel's voice is choked with emotion.

Diane crosses to Rachel and leads her to the front door. As she does, Diane attempts to sort out her emotions enough to say something pure, to express her love for her daughter stripped finally of ambiguity and resentment.

But there isn't time. On the front stoop, they stare at one another for a moment. Then Rachel is gone. A figure on the sidewalk getting smaller, disappearing at last into the fog pooling unseasonably at the bottom of the hill.

✦ ✦ ✦

They meet with Rachel a few times more. The conversation is always strained, Kyle saying little but refraining from making outbursts. He paces around the living room instead—adjusting paintings or items misaligned by the housekeeper's dusting. By the middle of June, there is no longer any word from her daughter. Rachel's cell and work phones are disconnected. Cards are returned when sent to her most recent address, the one in Austin. Diane phones her mother for information, but as always Elaine's responses are cheerily vague.

Diane, Kyle and Jason return to their lives. Drinks on the deck at six thirty, then dinner. Sometimes Diane spends the rest of the evening with the boys—a board game, a little TV—then slips out the back.

She begins work at last on the rear garden, hiring a pimply-faced neighbor boy on the weekends to help with the heavy tasks. She continues her volunteer shifts at the museum, the hospice, the helpline. She even makes peace with Robert, who from time to time hangs out in the call room just to tease her and have a laugh.

In October, when the shadows lengthen and the days grow warm, she receives a long-overdue letter from her mother. Diane's father, the indomitable C.K. Turner, is dying. Colon cancer. For over two years. Rachel is there with her now, Elaine writes. The big house doesn't feel so lonely anymore. Elaine says she would have revealed all this earlier, but she wanted someone in the family to be happy. If not her and her granddaughter, then Diane and Kyle.

Diane opens her hand, allowing the letter to float to her writing desk. Outside the window of the coach house, under a clear blue sky, the downtown office towers are gleaming.

Diane should go, be with her mother in her father's final hours. Doesn't she do that every week for people at the hospice? But she is not of that place anymore. Texas. She would let Rachel go. She would let Rachel go in her stead.

Jason

TWO QUICK TAPS at Jason's front door, followed by three slow ones. So familiar now, this promise of a shoulder to cry on, a good home-cooked meal for a change. He leaps from the kitchen table to answer it, but halfway up he lets himself fall back into his chair. He is not in a hurry anymore. A sip of coffee, then he focuses his attention on lowering his mug to the table through a shaft of dust-moted morning light. He inhales deeply before rising to his feet. One.

Kendall, the perky half of the young neighbor couple, is on the landing outside his door. Dressed in blue jean cut-offs, her curly black hair spills over a sage-green crop top.

"This came to our place yesterday." On the tip of one finger she balances the narrow FedEx tube by its end cap and floats it into Jason's grasp. "Sorry. I totally spaced it," she says.

Cradling the package in one hand, he attempts to assay its weight, along with the intensity of the next few days' work.

"Got time for coffee?" he says. "I have those blueberry scones you like."

"You actually went shopping?"

"I can provide for myself on occasion, darling." Jason grins, moving aside. He motions down the entryway with his free hand.

"I'm kind of buried at the moment in potato salad and coleslaw. And you *are* coming over, Mister. It's supposed to warm up later. And everybody's asking where you've been."

"Everybody?"

"Oh, you know. The usual suspects."

On the cardboard carton, Jason taps out a syncopated beat with the pads of his fingertips. "It appears I've gotten my marching orders, dear."

"It's Sunday, Jason. Come on. We're setting up the volleyball net. Sean's even grilling. He scored some killer steaks from a restaurant client."

"Sean? Cook?"

"I know. Right? That's why you *have* to come. Moral support and all. Besides, Matt will be there."

Matt, Sean's handsome and gregarious coworker.

"He's crushing on you, you know," she says, raising her eyebrows twice quickly, her smile turning loopy, slightly lopsided.

"He's a little out of my league, Kendall. Plus, I'm way too old."

"Apparently he doesn't think so."

"I'm just not up to socializing, sweetheart."

She cocks her head slightly and examines him, her curls draping onto one shoulder. "Are we having a bad day?"

Almost imperceptibly, Jason shrugs and frowns.

"Did you hear some news?" she says, the pitch of her voice rising, registering sympathy. "Something from Kyle?"

The wayward Kyle. He eloped to San Juan five years ago on a perfect spring day, just like this one, and joined Rebeca, his Puerto Rican benefactor and best pal.

"No. Not since that email three weeks ago."

"That house they're building down there does look nice."

"The point is—I'm not living in it."

"But he said you could visit, right?"

"Invitation rescinded. He says he needs some space."

"That fucking song and dance. Had a bunch of ex-boyfriends pull that crap on me."

"Any of them end up coming back?"

"Oh, honey. You're not still hoping for that, are you?"

"Depends on the day."

The coils of hair on Kendall's forehead begin to dance, the spring breeze from Muir Beach gusting suddenly. She wraps her arms around herself against the chill. "I saw you had a friend over last night."

"Are you snooping on me?" Jason says, smiling broadly.

"Beats watching soccer on ESPN with Sean."

"Doorbell trade."

"What?"

"Wasn't a friend. A hookup. Met him on that new smart-phone app."

"Well, that's progress, isn't it?"

"I started crying halfway into it and he fled."

"Okay, but still…"

"Yeah, I guess."

"And you're working again. That's good."

"Kendall, it's too early for one of your pep talks. Thanks for the mail."

Kendall's smile droops; she clutches herself more tightly.

Jason turns to go, but the guilt over his old mean-spiritedness dogs him. "I'm sorry, honey. You know I love your pep talks, right?"

Kendall lets her hands fall to her sides. Behind her, the box elder along the creek have at last leafed out, their pale-green tremblers rustling in the ocean breeze. "Okay, I'll let you get to work. Shall I bring you over a plate later?"

"Please, mommy."

Kendall draws the back of a finger down his cheek. "Such a baby."

Balling one hand and snugging it under his chin, Jason scrunches up his face. "Waah," he says, then breaks into a laugh.

Kendall turns her head slightly in the direction of her house. "I think my other baby's calling. You know, Sean. As a trial run, my husband is threatening to grill a steak for breakfast. I better get back before he burns the place down."

Jason pecks Kendall on the cheek, then tracks her bouncy gait through the line of eucalyptus trees, the border between their two properties.

He tosses the mail tube onto the layout desk in his office on his way to the kitchen. There, he knocks back the last of the cold coffee, grabs the garden tote from its station by the door, then heads outside.

From the deck, the electric-green lawn spills down the hill to the raised beds he installed the previous fall. Nested in a subdivision on a spur of Mount Tamalpais, his property is far enough from the road for the beach traffic not to bother him.

Again, he breathes in deeply. One. After exhaling through his nostrils, he takes another breath. Two. He continues, counting his inhalations up to ten like they taught him at the Zen practice center down the road.

Desperate and sad one day, he'd felt compelled there, down that twisty two-lane blacktop. Despite his ambivalence about his heritage on his mother's side of the family, he was shocked by what he saw. By all the people pretending to be Japanese, floating around the practice center in long black robes, bowing and chanting. Despite this, he found it calming—sitting quietly in the dark, cavernous assembly hall, the drumming, the bells. After avoiding its strangeness for months, he damped his antipathy to the place and wound his way back down the road repeatedly to park himself on a black, pill-shaped meditation pillow.

The dour teacher, the hair shorn on her stubbly head, admonished him in a private session to merge with his breathing and sit inside his grief over Kyle's abandonment. The more Jason did this—kneading himself into a pretzel on the pillow, his legs and lower back screaming—the more intense the experience of grief became. In the last few months, though, it had begun finally to fade.

Then he received Kyle's email about the house in San Juan he and Rebeca are breaking ground on this summer. The drawings he attached—those physical manifestations of Kyle's decision not to return to San Francisco, to Jason— were a gut punch rekindling the sensation of grief. Full force now, again scouring his whole body. As if his skin is being peeled away by something that is everywhere and nowhere at once. The background radiation left over from the Big Bang, say, only amped up times a million.

He steps onto the silky grass and surveys his refuge. Banks of dark-leafed rhodos heavy with white spring blossoms. Beds of gray sage, soon to be massing with purplish-blue petals. Behind them, sweet bay and redwood tumbling up a rocky spur of the mountain. And, farther along, motion-lessly arcing toward the summit, a hawk with its wings outspread against a blue sky.

For a year now, he has called all this home, since the house closed that he and Kyle shared with Diane on Potrero

Hill. With his only a third portion, he wasn't able to buy much in this tony neighborhood—just an acre lot with a two-story box sided with wooden shakes.

He ambles over to the raised bed closest to the house and lays down his tote. Under a clear sky, past the ridgelines to the west, he has a clean shot to the head of the valley. To the south, the green slope descends in fits and starts to the bay.

He tenses, an image flashing in his mind. Diane scowling down at her own view of the bay from the Potrero Hill house, which she now owns entire and lives in solo, treating it as a museum to her dear departed son.

One, he says to himself, inhaling a quick breath. Two, he says, gulping down another. Still, Diane's face swings back into view. Under her bright forelock, the dull brassy hair shot through with white, her face is flushed, contorted in anger. "You did this," it says.

He peels back the plastic netting and examines the sets he bedded last week, the spring weather finally warm enough to free them from their germination trays and grow lamps. Following an urge that came over him unexpectedly, he's put in plants his grandmother grew in her garden in Chico before she got too creaky to wield a spade—neat rows of tiny sprouted edamame and mizuna. Aubergines and daikon.

Jason's mother is a harried academic prone to takeout or microwaving their family's meals. And though his Polish

179

granddad was a real meat-and-potatoes guy, while Jason's Japanese gram was alive she would often prepare her old family recipes. When these vegetables ripen, he'll try his hand again at a few of them. Grilling the eggplant to a miso-glazed perfection, braising the white root in savory stock. *Nasu Dengaku, daikon no nimono*—words that have long ago lost their meaning but that remind him still of home.

He strips the yellowing leaves from the base of a few stems, jimmies a spading fork under the persistent weeds and lifts them from the soil. Out of the blue, he wonders what Kyle's sister is doing. It's been two weeks since he emailed Rachel with the news of her brother's fucking house. She's yet to reply—too busy, he supposes, now she's a successful author.

In the last fourteen years she's published four books under some pen name—an action/adventure series. Not that he wants to read them, really, but he still presses her for copies or, at least, the author name. She writes back how they're trash; that she won't insult his intelligence. They were selling well, though. He was happy for her.

He and Rachel have fallen into a fitful correspondence over the years. First on Facebook, where she has one of those lurker accounts—only two friends, him and some buxom Russian woman who was obviously running a scam. About a year after Rachel returned to Dallas to help with the care of her grandfather, they began communicating instead by email.

Hers were always brief, funny. A little snarky. When Jason couldn't travel to Dallas with Kyle and Diane for the grandfather's funeral, Jason emailed Rachel his condolences. Her reply: *Shit happens. On the plus side, no more bed pans.*

Years later, Jason pinged her to say how sorry he was that her grandmother, Elaine, now had the cancer. The response: *The old broad needs to kick it, already. Got my hands full with my ditzy dad.*

Five years ago, shortly after Kyle decamped, when Elaine finally succumbed, he received an email with an attachment. A vintage postcard of a bikini-clad pinup girl, clueless to the alligator behind her about to shred her ass. The text underneath: *I'm fine, thanks for asking. Moving to sunny fucking Fort Lauderdale with what's left of my dad.*

A month later, Jason fired off a long, self-pitying email to her about Diane. How Kyle's mother blamed Jason for her son opting out of returning from his visit to Puerto Rico. Jason figured, if anyone could sympathize with his plight, it would be Rachel. Instead, he got: *Well, friend, now you know how I felt.*

Though frequently like a kick in the ass, he grew fond of these emails. With Kyle's radio silence, after his rift with Diane, they were Jason's last remaining connection to the family that had once meant so much to him.

At Kendall and Sean's, somebody yells *Cannonball!* then there's a thump followed by the sound of water splashing. Then the sweet smell of marijuana floating in the air.

His new smartphone vibrates in his pocket. Company phone, now that he's summoned the wherewithal to go full-time again, albeit working three days a week from home. It is a text from the team designer, reminding Jason of the quick turnaround required on the sketches they just delivered.

He folds the netting back down and heads to the house. He'll put in a couple of hours, then go to Kendall and Sean's when everyone is well and truly baked. He isn't ready yet for a romantic complication, but he'll see about this Matt.

On the desk in his office is a computer and two large displays. He slices open the package with an X-Acto blade and unthreads the vellum sheets. This designer is old-school, loosely sketching by hand perspective drawings, rough building elevations. Jason's task is to turn them into a complete set of measured drawings—plans, sections, elevations—for the production team to consult when creating the construction documents. He's nothing more than a glorified draftsman, when once he was the firm's top designer. He's not ready for that kind of complication either.

Attached to the sketches is the design brief. Though his firm specializes in large commercial projects, they sometimes design residences for their client companies' top brass. This one is a beach house on Catalina. The sprawling ten-thousand-square-foot affair, with its deep verandas and porte cochere, is an overstuffed version of the house Kyle and Rebeca are building in San Juan.

In what has become a familiar act of self-flagellation over the last three weeks, Jason wakes his computer and pulls up Kyle's pencil sketches of the house. A couple of houses, really—one each for Rebeca and Kyle. As they do every time Jason views them, the drawings take his breath away. For Kyle has shaded not houses so much as his vision of a fully realized life.

In a detail view, down at the end of the long lanai that connects the two homes, a hammock drapes languidly from its supports. A figure reclines there in silhouette, one arm cascading from the netting's arc and lit up in a patch of sun.

In another, in the garden separating the two houses, someone—perhaps it is Kyle—reads in the shade of two tree ferns' broad fronds.

There's an evening scene by the pool. Under a nimbus of towering clouds, a dinner table set for ten, judging by the clustered wineglasses sparkling in the torchlight. On the second floor of the house, sheltered under the eaves that overhang the lanai, bright windows frame shadowed guests, roughly suggested in quick penciled marks.

And in an overall perspective—hemmed in on top by the rim of a striped umbrella, at the bottom by the tip of a towel and a stretch of sand—the building seems, not an intrusion on the beachscape, but an outgrowth of the embankment that embraces it.

Witnessing these drawings again, a nostalgia sweeps through Jason for this place he has never been. And the house plans deal their last smarting jolt. Ruled on the ground floor of Kyle's house, a master bedroom and, under the walkways above that overlook the garden, two rooms labeled *studio*.

There has never been even a suggestion that Jason join Kyle permanently in San Juan and this little detail caused the computer screen to blur when Jason first saw it. Tears flowing, he then finally removed his ring. There was no longer any use in pretending. It wasn't even a legal marriage anyway.

Jason closes the email containing the drawings and sends it to trash. An empty gesture. The images of the house are burnished in his mind now.

One, he counts silently, breathing in. Two. After meditating nearly a year, Jason is able to create distance now, however small and short-lived, from his anger and grief. And work, also, will take his mind off them this morning.

Jason logs on to the company server, fires up his CAD program. Before he begins, he checks his email. Still nothing from Rachel. Just junk. And an invitation from a senior VP requesting Jason join the firm's contingent at the AIA conference in October. It's a ploy, obviously, meant to lure their star designer further out of his hidey-hole. The offer is generous—all expenses paid, no responsibilities, a fat per diem. Even so, Jason is about to nuke the email when he notes the conference's location. Tampa. Florida.

✦ ✦ ✦

THE HEAT—still brutal here at the beginning of October—radiates through tinted windows into the air-conditioned interior of Jason's rental car. He navigates the SUV through Fort Lauderdale's twisty residential streets. Seagulls wheel and churn against a sky dotted with fair-weather clouds that are puffed up like his grandmother's green tea meringue.

The TomTom he rented on the dash orders him to turn left in five hundred feet. Heeding the command, he crosses a bridge onto one of the narrow man-made islands that make up the neighborhood of Lauderdale Harbors. Ahead, the blacktop threads between tall foxtail palms, each crowned with a riotous green bouquet. Their smooth trunks undulate in the convection waves coming off the pavement.

When he first emailed Rachel proposing a visit after his architecture conference, Jason was met with silence. All spring, between days at work or hanging out over at Kendall and Sean's, he peppered Rachel with requests. In June came her typical sarcastic reply: *Why bother?* In July, she wrote: *Up to my eyeballs here. Is there something you want?* He wasn't sure. It was only that he feels weirdly related to Rachel, if not by blood, then by sorrow. He wrote back: *Come on. It'll be fun.* More like ripping off a bandage after the wound has healed. Painful, but necessary.

Jason punches the brake when the GPS unit informs him he's reached his destination. Two large palm trunks protrude from the gravel in front of a small circular drive. Beyond that, a modest cream-colored, one-story stucco house, the window and door trim painted teal to match the plane of the fake tile roof.

Jason nudges his Ray-Bans back up to the bridge of his nose and steps outside. Instantly, sweat seeps from his pores; humidity binds his knit shirt to his skin. As he crosses the drive, his running shoes stick to snaky black patches of asphalt.

His finger trembles as it reaches for the doorbell. A dog barks. A rustling in the house. The trembling runs down his whole body as the door opens the length of its chain.

"Yeah?" The voice is deep, raspy—not what he expected—wariness in the rise of its inflection.

Jason is used to this, growing up in Chico in California's Central Valley, practically the only Asian. He's never denied his ancestry, but he doesn't broadcast it either. Despite that, on the occasions when he failed to pass, people there often acted mistrustful until they succumbed to his good-guy charms. "Rachel?"

"Yes?"

"It's Jason Stewart."

The chain clatters out of its channel. The door creaks. From the opening, a black-and-tan terrier barks at him, dancing excitedly, the little claws tapping the stone tiles in the entryway.

"Nippy, no!" Rachel shouts, bending down to wag one commanding finger at the little dog. It whimpers and shifts onto its haunches. "Jason? Wow, it's you. Sorry, I wasn't expecting you until next week."

He barely recognizes her because of her bulk that balloons the dirty lime-green sweats. She emits an odor of cigarettes and mouthwash. Long, limp hair clings to her pale face.

"It's the sixth," Jason says, "like we planned."

"What? Oh, shit. I wrote it down as the sixteenth. I'm such a dunce!"

"I can come back later."

"No, no. Come in."

When she leads him into the corridor, the dog begins a sequence of sharp yaps, each one like a nail driven into his skull. Rachel scoops up the terrier and tosses it onto an unmade bed in the adjoining room then slams the door shut.

On the coffee table in the living room, beer cans and half-empty wineglasses have corralled a plate of desiccated appetizers. Ashtrays brim with cigarette butts on the tall tables either side of a blood-red couch.

"Sorry the place is such a wreck. And me. I'm just getting up. Last night I had my mystery writers group over. Wait here half a sec, will you?" She pads in her bare feet into the bedroom. From behind the closed door, the dog begins to yap again.

Unsure what to do, Jason remains standing in the center of the living room. In an alcove to one side, on a dining table—pens of different colors bristling from a US Army mug, a laptop and, across the width of the table, rows of paper, neatly clipped in sections.

Above the sofa, a faded American flag crinkles behind glass in a metal frame. In another, set on the mantel above the fireplace's dusty ceramic logs, is a photo of a sad-looking soldier with a thick mustache. Army, enlisted man in dress blues, his cap canted rakishly across his forehead.

Jason steps to the mantel to examine the angular jawline— so familiar, too, the deep-set eyes. Next to the portrait, a medal dangles from a clear plastic frame.

"Dad won't have that at the old folks' home."

Jason jumps, startled by the brassy voice behind him. Standing in the opening to the hall, Rachel exhales cigarette smoke from taut lips. Her hair is pulled into a ponytail. She wears loose khaki shorts, a collared shirt whose bright pink clashes with her lipstick. The terrier sits on his hind legs beside her and growls.

"The Purple Heart, that is," Rachel says. "Dad thinks somebody at the home where he lives will steal it. Personally, I think he doesn't want to be reminded of who he used to be."

The little dog sidles up at Jason's feet and sniffs his pants leg while Jason scrutinizes again the photo of the father. He searches for the monster Kyle described, but all Jason can see is their resemblance. Not just in the structure of the face, but in the sadness of the eyes, the fatigue suggested by the drooping lids, the crow's-feet furrowing the flesh.

"Pretty startling, how much they look alike, don't you think?" Rachel says.

"How old was he then?"

Rachel crosses the room and, cigarette dangling from her lips, lifts the photo off the mantel and examines the back. "Nineteen ninety-two. Must have been taken right after my mother quit him. He'd be, what? Forty-eight?"

"Kyle's age."

"The coincidences pile up."

"What?"

"Don't mind me. Occupational habit. I'm always trying to find connections. Speaking of … Check this out."

Rachel saunters to the bookshelf next to the opening to the dining area. She runs her index finger down a neat row of identical-looking books. She tilts one forward, slips it out and tosses it to Jason.

Under the book's banner, *Rough Justice*, is a soldier who looks nearly identical to Kyle in a photo from fetish night at the Loading Dock. His long hair laps his shoulders. Dog tags nest between the mounds of his chest on a white tank top that veers into loose camo pants. Only this man on the cover sports a missile launcher on one shoulder, a bandolier with a neat row of ammo diagonally across his torso. A downed helicopter ablaze in the background, the soldier holds the hand of a chimpanzee, who gazes up at him adoringly. The title under the painting reads: *Operation Bonobo Rescue*.

"I snagged that photo of Kyle off your Facebook page. Kind of an homage to my dad, too, whose chopper got smoked in Nam."

Jason begins to leaf through the book. Rachel snatches it from his hand, but not before he notices the dedication: *To Jason, for trying.*

"You don't want to read that crap." She snaps the book shut, sticks it back on the bookshelf in the gap between the spines. She winces, with two fingertips massages tiny circles into the skin at her temple. "How about a cocktail?"

"Serious?"

"Deadly. I need a drink. A little hair of the dog. Plus, if we're going to get into all this, both of us probably could use one."

IN THE KITCHEN, the sun casts a yellow parallelogram onto the linoleum in front of the paired sliding doors. Rachel draws vertical blinds across them, carving dark slices into the skewed yellow box on the floor. She glances at the wall clock, something like guilt fleetingly washing across her face. It is barely noon.

The lit end of her cigarette hisses in the brown liquid in the bottom of the ashtray, where lipstick-stained filters stew. "My drink's Jack and Coke. How about a beer?"

While she fixes the drinks, Jason feels suddenly jittery. Despite the little speech he rehearsed all morning driving across the Everglades from Tampa, he really hasn't a clue what to say to her. He takes short, quick breaths to counter the feeling of being suffocated in the tightly sealed room. Overpowering the must from the air-conditioning vents is the smell of cigarette smoke, of the ashtray's rancid pool.

He flings open the door and steps outside. Slipping the Ray-Bans from his shirt collar, he puts them on to ward off the harsh light. The heat of the sun scours his face, his bare forearms, masking for a moment that irradiated sensation of his grief.

He stares off past the blue kidney-shaped pool—past the dark water shimmering with bright-yellow shards—to the mansions on the adjacent island at the far side of the narrow channel.

Behind him, a clattering of vertical blinds. The sliding door whispers in its track. "Nippy?" Rachel says. "Want to come out? No? Suit yourself, kid." Rachel slams the glass panel on the little charcoal-and-brown face, then marches across the patio in a wide side-to-side gait. "Apologies," she says. "I know how particular you San Francisco boys are about your beer."

Jason grabs the Bud, the metal can already blistering with condensation.

"Come on," she says. "The hefty gal needs to sit."

Jason follows her to a patio table shielded from the water behind a screen of fan palms and shaded by a large red umbrella. At the sliding doors, the terrier wriggles his head between the white slats and watches from behind the glass.

Rachel lowers herself into a molded white plastic chair, places the iced drink against her temple. "That runt's smarter than we are. I'm about to pop a gasket in this heat. Seems fall will never arrive, here in sunny South Florida. I mean, it's friggin' October already."

Retrieving a BIC from the pocket of her shorts, she lights another cigarette. She wags it in the direction of the plastic chair opposite her and Jason sits. He swigs the beer. "That's your grandfather's name, isn't it?" he says. "The author of those books."

"Yup. C.K. Turner. I'm not that imaginative. I've got to take my material wherever I find it. I've two more series on the go now. One by Elaine Lancaster. That's a riff on my grandmother's name. Another by Tiana Brewster, after my best friend in Killeen. Who knows? Maybe I'll give you a real Japanese-sounding last name and do some Asian super-spy shit."

Jason snorts a laugh into his half-empty beer can.

Rachel scrutinizes the fan palm tassels waving in the breeze at the tip of each accordion pleat. Jiggling her leg, she considers him for a moment out of the corner of her eye. "So, just wondering. How does Kyle like being Rebeca's butt-boy?"

Here is the snarky Rachel he's grown fond of over the years. Ironically funny, never bothering to play nice. Still, the bluntness of the question makes him feel suddenly defensive. "It's not like that. More of a win-win, I think.

She handles the financing, acquires the land for them to develop. He gets to do what he loves."

She blows a skein of smoke away from him. "Like designing that fucking house. What a monstrosity."

"I was surprised," he says, his fingers lightly cinching the can and rotating it on the tabletop. "It's actually kind of nice."

"Thought you hated it."

"I'm just glad he's designing finally. It frustrated him, mostly being on the technical side."

"Saint fucking Jason, all of a sudden."

"I've had the whole summer to get over myself about that house."

The tip of Rachel's cigarette crackles and blooms red. In a cloud of smoke, she eyes him again slightly askance. "Okay, I get Kyle's got a sweet deal down there, but to ditch you and my mother without warning? Seems pretty harsh. You ever get a bead on why he did it?"

This is a question that was long unfathomable. The years right before Kyle scampered off, he appeared to be doing so well. His handsome, overpaid psychiatrist finally dialed in Kyle's medication. Though Kyle complained of there being a flattening of his emotions, Jason found it preferable to his hiding under the covers all day or gazing blankly at the ceiling.

Kyle's professional life, too, had finally gelled. He made it into a big downtown architecture firm, despite his lack of academic credentials. Though he considered his new position to be a validation of his self-worth, Kyle fretted over there being no longer any call for his illustrations in the tightly regimented organization.

The answer, Jason now understands, is in Kyle's sketches of the San Juan house. They codify what Kyle told him over a long, late night Skype call a month after he arrived in Puerto Rico.

In San Juan, Kyle explained, he was a different person. He had a full complement of feelings. Joy when the pencil again sketched a fresh page. He felt centered by the sound of waves pulsing outside his window. There was a fluidity to his movements, his body buoyed by the salt water that licked his skin. And there was the language, the music that now more readily flowed from his lips. There was passion too, around a dinner table bathed in sunsets. Deep conversation, not catty pop culture commentary or amped-up political sermonizing.

He flushed his antidepressants down the toilet, Kyle said, his image beaming happily on Jason's computer screen. For the first time in his life, he said, he felt relaxed.

That Skype call was their final moment of intimacy, one that was replaced by the flurry of emails and texts that diminished over the years. He's shared Kyle's drawings of the house with Kendall and Rachel, but, not wanting to weaken its hold on him, he's walled this conversation off in his mind, where it provides sanctuary to the last remnant of his time with Kyle. And, though Rachel deserves an

194

explanation, her family's motivations so long mysterious, he balks at giving it to her now. This safe haven he will withhold and keep to himself.

Jason swishes the beer at the bottom of the can, knocks back the bitter liquid. "I don't know. Seems like running away from things is just in Kyle's nature."

Rachel hammers her cigarette out in the ashtray on the table. "Boy, you had me hyped up here, coming all this way. I was expecting some big reveal. You mean to tell me this is *all* you got? *It's in his nature?* Like I don't already fucking know this?"

"It's not that complicated, Rachel. He's happy. He got a better offer."

"Little shit."

"Excuse me?"

"I'm not talking about you." Rachel cocks her head back and drains her glass. It makes a sharp crack when she lowers it to the nubby plastic tabletop. "Why did you come here, Jason? We've only seen each other a handful of times in fourteen years. Emails—what?—four, five a year."

"I always felt we had a connection. Especially now."

"Now that we've both been dumped by Kyle, you mean. It's not a club I ever wanted to belong to. But evil deeds beget violent acts. I figure you know all about that too now."

"You think I did this?"

"I may be going out on a limb here. But those times I came to your house and you were bickering with Kyle, I thought, what the heck? I'd have given my left nut to have what you had. Metaphorically speaking."

"I'm pretty sure I was defending *you*."

"Sure, and I appreciate that. But did you ever stop to think that my mother might be at least a little bit right?"

Jason's fingers close around the thin metal, crumpling the can.

"You know," Rachel says, "about her blaming you for running Kyle off."

"And?"

"And nothing. Shit happens. Own up to it, champ. You play the heavy for fucking once. It must be exhausting—always having to be the nice guy."

Jason jerks up in his chair. "I love your biting emails, but in person, not so much."

Rachel spreads her arms wide, palms forward, fingers splayed. "This is me, Jason. Take it or leave it."

"What a fucking idiot I am! I remembered you being so timid and sweet at the house. I figured I'd come here, we'd have some *kumbaya* thing, get all misty about Kyle. What happened to you, Rachel?"

"News flash, Jason. My mother and Kyle treating me like shit for something I did when I was only twelve. Wiping my grandparents' asses for years and none of you lifting a finger to help. So, in brief, motherfucker, you happened. You and your whole little shit show."

Rachel is leaning forward, having yelled all this at Jason. The terrier barks furiously. Standing on its hind legs, pawing the sliding door, its claws clatter against the glass.

There is a churning inside Jason—sudden, prickly, inchoate. He bolts to his feet, drops the can to the concrete patio, smashes it under the heel of his tennis shoe. "You know what? Screw you. I don't need this." He wheels around, strides to the side gate. He slams it shut behind him and stalks off.

Over his shoulder, the sound of a plastic chair skittering across the pad, then Rachel, calling his name.

✦ ✦ ✦

Jason is powering down his anger, through the spindle of sand that connects the communities south of Fort Lauderdale. He's heading to the beach. Like Kyle, to be soothed by the rhythm of waves, the cool salt spray on his skin. To wash away this terrible feeling, this combined betrayal—mother, brother, sister, son. Husband. Better not hit the sand in Fort Lauderdale, though. Or even Miami Beach. Better get as far away from that crazy woman as he can.

Soon, the upscale properties on either side of the road peter out and are replaced by scattered cheap motels that are, in turn, replaced by the hotel and apartment canyons of Miami Beach. He doesn't stop there to admire the Art Deco beauties—formerly run-down, with gray-hairs perched on metal chairs ornamenting their verandas, now boutique hotels with hipster bars and wannabe starlets rollerblading out front. He doesn't stop downtown to admire the vaunted Miami-style architecture, the planes of stark colors, the audacious forms.

He craps out finally at two in the afternoon, parking near the water on a little patch of brush and sand across from a boat club. The sun sinking into the Gulf blasts over the dashboard and wakes him. He threads the chain of beach towns along Route 1—the scrub islands strung along the archipelago, the little saltwater coves—arriving just before ten in boy-crazy Key West.

All this time Rachel is calling him. At least he assumes it's her. Every half hour, his cell phone washes the interior of the SUV with an eerie blue glow, the display lit up with a Fort Lauderdale number. How Rachel got his, he doesn't know. He'd withheld that from her as well, fearing, with good reason it seems, that their meeting might prove problematic.

And why are these women in his life so damn difficult?

Rachel he understands. But he doesn't take any pleasure in his role as collateral damage. Nor does he with Diane back in San Francisco, who is petty and retributive, combative when she should be a solace to him, as he would be to her.

Then there's Kyle's *Rebequita*—her coal-black hair, the devilish beauty mark on her cheek, her saucy laugh—solicitous to Jason back in San Francisco. But unapologetic, he thinks in these unkind moments, for the many nights she kidnapped Kyle at her house—spoon-feeding him Spanish lessons, hatching her evil plans.

Jason wishes he were home now. Not Chico. Jason long ago left the small-mindedness of his childhood home, his parents, both academics at the state university. His Japanese-American mother, a loving but demanding presence. His white father, not abusive like Kyle's, just petty, self-satisfied.

No, he wishes he were in his little box of a house on the slope of Mount Tam. Stretched out on his living room couch, the light of the setting sun slanting in, his head on Kendall's lap. She would be stroking his hair now. They would be laughing, going over their crazy day.

He parks the car in front of his B and B, set in a quiet neighborhood far from rowdy Duval Street. He'll check in in the morning. Now, what he needs is a whole lot of rowdy.

Though it's the shoulder season, the sidewalks down here on Duval—fronting T-shirt shops, restaurants and bars—are swarming with boozy partiers. A group of college kids gathers under an arch of the baroque facade of the San Carlos, slyly passing around a silver flask. Catty-cornered across the street, a rock band is playing "Margaritaville" in the patio of Willie T's. And farther along Duval, stationed on a side street, is a fleet of Key West's ubiquitous bikes.

It is disorienting how familiar this all is. Other than the name change of some restaurants, the place is as the one frozen in his memory. When he spies himself reflected in the storefront at the Gap, he expects to find a man in his twenties, not the forty-year-old going to seed in the glass.

At a food cart, he wolfs down a couple of hot dogs. Then, just as he knew he would, two blocks up he locates it: the same shabby one-story building, the same black metal grates over windows and doors, the bedraggled rainbow flag drooping out front.

He pushes through the black vinyl that curtains the entrance. Inside the narrow room, positioned on stools at the long bar, is a row of mostly shirtless men—retirees, judging by the gray hair and paunch, traveling on the cheap before the winter hordes descend.

Above the bottles of booze at the mirrored bar, a headless mannequin swims through a maelstrom of copper coils. Jason feels as if he's being sucked into a whirlpool of his own, one of blame and self-pity.

Rachel is right to be angry about his withholding. Right also about his and Kyle's fights. Though they weren't arguments so much—just Jason popping off while Kyle stared blankly out the window or at the ceiling. What she hasn't seen, though, are the in-between times. Sunday mornings—their bodies radiant, exhausted after having sex—lolling in bed napping, reading the *Chronicle*. Or spooning on the grass under a limpid azure sky—a break from hiking up Mount Tam—huddled together there against the chill winnowing off the Pacific. And later, after the fog returns its comforting blanket of mist, a quiet dinner in the nook by the fireplace at the Pelican Inn. The ordinariness of these events thrills him, bringing a feeling so sublime he bursts into tears whenever they are recalled.

Jason signals the bartender. Blue light from the over-head fixtures shimmers on his polished head. His chiseled torso is trussed in a leather harness, nipples encircled by silver rings that connect the black straps. He hands Jason a beer bottle and winks. This triggers the familiar sensation—a pressing heaviness in his arms and legs, a surging outward, paired with a deep, unbreachable longing.

Men lean aggressively against the wall or else shout at each other in groups, the clamor competing with the deafen-ing music, a pulsing heartbeat. Jason slams the beer—too sweet by half—and barks for another. He glowers in a dark corner. Nobody dares approach him. At 2 a.m., when some nearby bars close, fresh troops occupy the room. They edge in on him, exacerbating an old fear dredged up in moments of weakness, that of being alone in a sea of white faces.

Through the crowd of these men, he catches sight of Kyle, or, in Jason's drunken state, a nearly perfect facsimile of him. It is a mental trick Jason often indulged in San Fran-cisco after his husband abandoned him, in a sudden rushed excitement on the subway spotting Kyle. Or on the street, his image aped by some aging muscle queen.

And here, propped against the wall at the far end of the long, dimly lit room. Only Jason comes to understand, when he saunters over and chats the man up, he is some kind of academic, like Jason's parents. In Key West for a conference, the man says—something no one ever is. Would you really travel to Sodom for continuing education credits?

While men skulk pass them, traversing the opening to the backroom, the man tells Jason he has a husband at home in Minneapolis. He raises his left hand to show off the oversized wedding band. So recently removed, Jason senses the ghost of his haunting the story the man tells. How he was raised on a farm in the Midwest—four hundred apple trees, some pears, a parcel by the river for alfalfa, but no stock. Pure happiness, he confesses with an embarrassed laugh, but so lonely. We were the lonely ones, he says. Weren't we? Us gay boys.

Jason considers this line of conversation unsuited for a sleaze bar. To shut the man up, Jason gives him a wolfish grin, a quick tilt of the head toward the backroom. In his sodden way of thinking, Jason hopes to destroy finally his attachment to Kyle by having sex there with his doppelgänger.

The dark room smells of stale beer and semen. Men couple and uncouple in a dull red light. Hanging in a sling in one corner is a potbellied, graying codger wearing only a cock ring and black leather boots. Someone groans in the shadows.

Jason presses into the man from Minneapolis and kisses him. Jason still finds it shocking kissing anyone other than

Kyle, even someone who is a dead ringer for him, as this man is. For a long time after Kyle took off, Jason wasn't able to manage even this, inhibited as he was by the ever-present background of his grief. But lately, sometimes Jason locates voids in this field that he can enter, where lust is a revolt from sorrow, sex with a stranger retribution for Kyle's abandonment. Often, though, midway through the act, the void will close, as it does now, with tears—Jason's kissing losing urgency, the power that skin has over him diminishing.

Sensing this, the man pulls away, then melts into the darkness. Jason allows invisible hands to grope him. With anonymity his scruples vanish in an unencumbered physicality. After he comes, he zips up and returns to the bar. There is no sign of the man he made out with.

Jason lingers over other beers until shortly before 4 a.m., when the bartender announces last call. Jason stumbles through Key West's shadowy streets past white clapboard houses. Their porch rails are filigreed, the windows framed at the sides by black shutters. Behind a white picket fence, enormous philodendron leaves float like the heads of dragons.

+ + +

IN THE DUSKY LIGHT, Jason plants his running shoes on the lowest of three steps. He collapses onto the concrete pad, his legs exhausted from holding their fixed position during the long early morning drive.

The previous night, after closing yet another bar, he stood on the pier at the end of Duval Street while around him couples made slurpy noises in the dark. After a while, to the east, across a blank expanse of water, under scattered stars broke the least little light. The tawdriness of the last few days suddenly disgusted him and, grabbing his bag from the B and B, he beat it back up the Keys to Rachel's door.

A chain rattles behind him; hinges squeak. He twists around to see Rachel, her face in a manuscript, stooped in the open doorway. She wears a pressed white Western shirt that she has long outgrown. Embroidered in floral filigrees, its front panels, puckered at the hems, are barely held together with mother-of-pearl snaps. Too-tight jeans tuck into a pair of new Tony Lama boots.

While she reads, she fishes with her free hand for the newspaper that leans in its orange liner against the door-frame. She snags it, stands and starts, her head lurching back. "Oh, I didn't hear the bell."

"I was just sitting here."

"You're pretty good at this yourself."

"What?"

"Running away."

"Look, you asked me to come. I came. What do you want?"

"Did you think this was over?"

Jason scrambles onto all fours, pushes off the lip of the landing and wobbles upright. He hitches onto the circular drive to cross the graveled yard to his rental car.

"You look like you could use some coffee," Rachel calls after him. "Pot's ready."

"Fine." Jason shakes his head side to side, making a display of his annoyance.

At the doorway, she pauses and looks back. In the opening, her terrier stands guard, grumbling lowly.

"I'm not going back in there," Jason says.

The corners of her mouth turn down, a puff of air escapes her nostrils. "How do you take it?"

"Black," he says. Turning his back on her, he crumples again onto the landing.

In front of him in the gathering light, steam rises from the palm tree–lined street, dampened by the thundercloud that let loose minutes before. He watches it move inland, a slumbering, tentacled giant pursued by armies of high cirrus.

"One coffee, black," Rachel says, returning to the concrete pad, accompanied by the chatter of tiny claws. She taps Jason's shoulder and hands him a mug. Positioned behind him, she takes in a long breath. "Smell that?"

"The coffee?"

"No, the after-it-rains smell. You can't describe it in words. I've tried. It's not a smell, really, but a memory."

"You ought to pull your head out of your ass every once in a while. Now would be good."

"Okay, look. I apologize for being such a bitch before. Obviously, I still haven't come to grips with all this. Plus, I'm under a lot of pressure. I've got three manuscripts to deliver by Thanksgiving and I'm worried about my dad."

"Oh?"

"I've got him in a nice place close by in Wilton Manors. They rang me right before you showed up to say he's acting crazy again. I mean, jeez, he's not even that old. What they call your early onset." She draws the cigarette tucked behind her ear and rolls it back and forth between her index finger and thumb. "So, I kind of lost it, what with being hungover and all. Plus, and this is just a me thing, I can come across pretty harsh if I think people can handle it."

"How's that working for you?"

Her laugh is deep, throaty, roughened over the years, he supposes, from too many cigarettes, too much Jack Daniel's.

"Not so hot," she says. "I mean, those mystery group gals are even saucier than I am. But I got eighty-sixed from my book club. Those petty petunias think I'm too opinionated."

"Book clubs," Jason says, screwing up his face in mock indignation. "Those deals are just an excuse to get together and drink. Personally, I don't need a cover."

Rachel laughs again, spilling her coffee. "Why, he *does* have a sense of humor after all." She places her mug on the landing then struggles to heave her bulk onto its lip. She retrieves the BIC from the coin pocket of her jeans and lights the cigarette.

The terrier takes up its post behind them and barks wildly.

"Nippy, shut the fuck up." Rachel torques around to swat the wet black nose. After another pull on the cigarette, she expels a shroud of acrid smoke.

Jason coughs, waving the cloud away with a flat hand.

"Oh, sorry," she says. "I'm just so used to smoking out here solo. Forgot my manners. While I'm on a roll, let me ask you this. Did you get laid out there?"

"Excuse me?"

"I mean, I always had the feeling you and Kyle were exclusive."

"Yeah, so?"

"I was just wondering how you were handling it now. I mean, that is still why people go to Key West, isn't it? The beaches there are pretty much crap."

"Yes, I did, if you're so goddam curious. As far as it goes."

"Don't get testy. We're just having a conversation."

She blows smoke above a bed of spent daylilies lined up against the front of the house. The sky brightens and the air grows warm. The terrier whimpers. Rachel jiggles her leg, sleeved tightly in blue denim.

"I know I gave you crap about it," Rachel says, "but you shouldn't listen to my mother. We've all had a hand in this.

Especially Kyle. She can't see that. She's always idolized him. Her guilt over the shit that went on in Texas."

Jason shuts his eyes. Fatigue bears down on him. He lists slightly away from Rachel, shoulders drifting downward to hang from his frame.

"You okay?" Rachel says.

"I'm just super tired. Didn't sleep last night."

Rachel drops the cigarette butt onto the lowest step, twists it out with the sole of her boot and brushes it onto the flower bed. "We'd be more comfortable inside, don't you think? I was about to make breakfast."

"How did you get my cellphone number?"

"I called my mother."

"That must have been interesting."

"We talk. Every now and then. And she still sends me postcards. Fewer now. She doesn't go anywhere to collect them."

"Then you didn't need my weepy email. You already knew Diane blamed me about Kyle."

Rachel traces a fingertip along the filigreed embroidery of her Western shirt. "She's a mess, Jason. You should call her. Pretend you're begging for forgiveness or something. She's too proud to ever apologize."

"Why would I do that? Diane hates me."

"By now, you ought to know this: The women in our family, we're just plain hard to deal with. Me. Mother, too. My grandmother, Elaine. Now, there was a real piece of work."

208

"I've been doing better lately. Except for the last few days. But mostly, I'm better. Resigned, I guess. To get into all this again with Diane? No, we had a good run, her, me and Kyle. But shit happens. Own it, right?"

"Okay, I did say that. But Jason, it's total crap."

He pours the last of the coffee and grinds onto the flowers. "You and me, Rachel, let's both just call it quits. All of this, your family stuff—it's ancient history."

"Ancient history? Yeah."

Rachel leans backward. Abruptly, she propels her upper body forward and, assisted by the momentum of her weight, in a graceful arc rises to her feet. The terrier scuttles out of her path as she strides to the open door. Jason twists around to watch her rummaging through her bedroom closet, tossing shoes and cardboard boxes on the floor. He extends his hand for the dog to sniff, but it backs away.

When Rachel returns, she has a beat-up cardboard box in her hands. The dog sidesteps away as she scrambles back onto the landing and sits. Next to the swoopy lines of his running shoes, her Tony Lamas look like bloated lizards.

She parks the box between them on the top step and nudges it toward Jason with the heel of her boot. "I'd completely forgotten about this."

The terrier wiggles in between them, flops onto the landing and nestles his chin onto crossed paws. Jason pulls back the torn flaps, releasing a musty smell into the humid morning. Lined up inside are the black spines of nearly thirty books. As he slips one out, a crumpled, yellowed sheet falls back into the box. Its edges darkened from handling, the page contains a pencil sketch of a teenaged Black boy with a broad nose and shaved head. His eyes are closed as if he is sleeping.

"I found them," Rachel says, "when I was clearing out Dad's house. Kyle must have forgotten them when he ran off to San Francisco in such a huff. Weird, Dad keeping them all those years."

"Especially this." Jason flips through pages and pages of naked men, some with flaccid penises, others with erections.

"Oh, yeah," Rachel says. "Especially that." She leans over, retrieves a stack of books from the box. Between them, the little dog yips when she squeezes in too close.

Rachel shuffles through the drawings. A jowly middle-aged man, doe-eyed and smiling. A boy with a thick spray of hair over a handsome, all-American-looking face. "Kyle was so good at this, even then. Shame he gave it up."

"He's started again, actually. Portraits of fishermen, he says. Vendors at the market. Locals from the neighborhood. I should have told you this before."

One eyebrow arches as Rachel purses her lips and nods. "Everybody in our family needed something back then to get us through that mess. Drawing was always it for him."

"How about you?"

"I don't know. Being a little shit, I guess." She slides a book from the bottom of her stack and pages through it. "Here it is."

The faces of two little girls sideways on the sheet, one lightly shaded, the other dark, their eyes starkly drawn to depict what appears to be too much makeup. A finely shadowed globe of bubblegum covers their lips.

"I wonder what happened to her," Rachel says, caressing with her thumb the edge of the paper. She riffles through more pages and stops. A portrait of a woman inching up on middle age stares up at them. A solitary pearl at each earlobe and a strand of the same at the open collar of her blouse. The date in the corner reads *1980*.

The resemblance to the woman Jason knows is barely discernible, not because of the difference in age—in the sketch she appears, if anything, even older.

"I didn't see it then," Rachel says, "but look, Kyle totally nailed it. I mean, I got that my mother was angry. I just didn't see how unhappy she was." Rachel pinches the corner of the page and turns to the next. "Now, this I did recognize."

A portrait of Kyle's father, about the same age as Diane in the previous sketch, mustache meticulously trimmed, hair buzzed short at the sides and flat on top. Seated in a plastic lawn chair, his head is cocked slightly and angled down, his shoulders hunched as if burdened by some great weight. Each gesture the epitome of Kyle.

Sunlit now in a brilliant amber, the crowns of the tall palms in Rachel's front yard rustle in a sudden gust. The trembling is taken up in succession by the fronds of each tree lining the narrow lane. The old feeling penetrates Jason's exhaustion, the background radiation of the universe scouring his skin. A prickly sensation, an incarceration of sorts, in the still middle of which is his grief. It has been overlain the last days with anger and booze and fumbling sex, and he has missed it. For through it he feels the presence of Kyle, so palpable this portion of being alive that was given Jason to know. His chest and abdomen tighten. The sobs come in waves, the animal moans.

Rachel places a hand on Jason's shoulder. He begins to recoil, then softens under her touch. One, he says to himself, breathing deeply. Two, he says on the next inhalation, his shoulders dropping, the muscles in his face beginning to relax.

He revels now in his grief, the scouring all over and through him. For, powerful as this irradiating sensation is and the feeling of Kyle it contains, he knows one day soon they will both dissipate. This awareness squares the loss, both for Kyle and now also for his shadow.

The sun crests over the ridgeline of Rachel's roof, casting dark angles across her pebbled yard. Larger shades intersect them, to glide across the blacktopped street then up and over the houses on the other side. A flock of twenty or so pelicans drifting low overhead on their way to feed in the open ocean, their wings flung stiffly at their sides, their gullets tucked under their big pointy beaks.

Rachel removes her hand from his shoulder. Using it to shield her eyes, she tracks the birds' slow flight. "Thank God," she says. "Summer is finally over."

It is hot now. Mist is rising off every hard surface, burning off the last traces of the rain. Jason wipes sweat mingled with tears from his temples. "How can you tell?"

"I don't know. There's just something about the light."

He peers at the birds, reaching down as he does to absent-mindedly massage the terrier behind one of its flappy ears. Flying higher now, the pelicans are silhouetted against a field of deep blue laced with milky threads. He tries, but he can't. He can't see what she sees.

He pivots around to face her. How out of place Rachel looks, sitting there with the tall palms in the background. Practically splitting the seams of that ridiculous Western getup, with Kyle's books piled on her lap. Like some husky but studious rodeo girl, a wallflower crashing somebody's luau.

"What?" she says. "You see something funny?"

"No."

"Then what are you grinning about?"

"Honestly, Rachel. At this point, who the fuck can say?"

She returns her stack of books to the box. Arching backward then throwing her weight forward, like an elegant ballerina she floats upright. Startled by the sudden maneuver, the little dog jumps into Jason's lap.

Balling her hands on her hips, Rachel cocks her head and laughs her raucous laugh. "You two," she says. "Ready to eat something, Jason?"

"Sure. I guess. Why not?" Cradling the dog in one arm, he cants backward and prepares to attempt her move. While the terrier squirms, Jason hurls his torso forward. Rising to an awkward-looking squat, Jason's tired legs spill him back onto the landing. The dog wriggles out of his grasp, trots over to the doorway and sits.

"Doofus," Rachel says.

Jason shoots her a pouty, theatrical smile. Offers her his hand. "Help me up, will you?"

Credits

Sections of this book were previously published in different forms as short stories.

Parts of chapter one appeared as "Approaching Zero" in *The Puritan: Frontiers of New English*, Issue 18, October 2012.

Parts of chapter three appeared as "A Momentary Lapse" in *Sanskrit Literary-Arts Magazine*, Vol. 43, June 2012.

Parts of chapter four appeared as "The Letter" in *Rougarou, An Online Literary Journal*, Vol. 8, Issue 2, January 2013.

Parts of chapter five appeared as "Approaching Zero" in *The Puritan: Frontiers of New English*, Issue 18, October 2012.

Parts of chapter six appeared as "Hit Me Back" in *Compass Rose*, Vol. XI, May 2011.

Acknowledgements

Writing is a solitary act. Still, none of us does it entirely alone. I've been extraordinarily blessed in creating this book. By Caroline Adderson's mentoring—her challenge to link and rework previously published stories, her believing in and supporting the resulting work. By my editor at Biblioasis, John Metcalf, who selected the work for publication and helped deepen it, urging me in the process to heed my inner novelist. By Nancy Zafris, whose early tough love and support allowed me to believe in myself as a writer. By the Biblioasis production team—managing editor Vanessa Stauffer, copyeditor John Sweet, and cover designer Ingrid Paulson—who sharpened the prose and crafted and promoted the beautiful object you hold in your hand. My eternal gratitude goes to the intrepid Biblioasis publisher, Dan Wells, for including me in his illustrious roster of authors.

I have also benefited from the discernment of my Alaskan partner-in-crime, Martha Amore, who has rescued many a story from impending disaster. My thanks go out as well to my fellow workshop and critique group members. Foremost among these are those in my Alaska writing groups, whose support and camaraderie I look back upon with great fondness. Included in this are the participants in four Kenyon Review Writers Workshops, a tremendously supportive writers summer camp where the second chapter of this book had its genesis. The input from these writers helped to shape early versions of these stories.

Thanks also to the literary journals who published them, whose brave work to support writers and the literary arts goes mostly unsung. Appearing in their pages spurred me on whenever my enthusiasm flagged for the difficult task of writing fiction.

My heartfelt appreciation goes out to my friends, who kindly suffered through my repeated prattle about writing and who supported me nonetheless.

Lastly, I am deeply indebted to my late husband, the Canadian visual artist and writer Alex Turner. Without him, I never would have fully understood love and loss, emotions core to the work. This and his reading and commenting upon draft after draft of stories without complaint has many times over earned him the dedication to this book.

LUCIAN CHILDS has been a Peter Taylor Fellow at the Kenyon Review Writers Workshop. He is a coeditor of Lambda Literary finalist *Building Fires in the Snow: A Collection of Alaska LGBTQ Short Fiction and Poetry*. Born in Dallas, Texas, he has lived in Toronto, Ontario, for fifteen years, since 2015 on a permanent basis.